D0865224

Daddy's Favorite Pop

A NOVEL
BY
ANTOINETTE SMITH

STTP Books
Riverdale, Ga.

678-694-1422
Vocal Coach

ISBN: 978-1-60743-697-3
Cover design by MarionDesigns.com

Printed in the United States of America
First Printing February 2009
10 9 8 7 6 5 4 3 2 1

A note from the author

Please don't judge my dad
Even though my parents' situation was sad
All my life, I knew how to deal with the pain
But I don't want this book to put my daddy to shame
What was done is in the past
Now all I want from him is a friendship that will last
The last time we spoke his words almost made me cry
The conversation we had was deep, I can't lie
But I assured him that this book would not end his life
Because everyone in the world has been through similar
things in their life
So, Daddy, if you read this book, all of it isn't true
I'm glad God helped me find you
My mom forgives you and so do I
Let's just give our relationship another try
Don't worry about what people say.
 Only God can judge you.

All you need to know is that I LOVE YOU!!!!

Upcoming titles by the author:

#LYPSTYCK DYKE
#WOMEN R DOGS 2
#I'M BI, Y LIE?
#WHITE COP, LIL' BLACK GURL
#I'M KEEPING HIM YOUNG
#BLACK-OUT ON BANKHEAD
#DIAMONDS (R A WHORE'S BEST FRIEND)
#MY LIFE, MY PAIN (BOOK OF POEMS)
#SHORT SIMPLE & SWEET (BOOK OF POEMS)

Chapter One
In the Beginning...

This is my life story as seen by many.

Mama was only fourteen when she had me. Daddy was twenty-six. When I was born, Mama told me that Daddy was very glad. I was the oldest of two. I had a brother who was one year younger than me.

We were born to Antonio Charles Watson, Sr. and Vurilyn Renae Sims. Mama told me that Daddy had gotten my name out of their names. My name is Tonae Ann Watson. My brother was named after Daddy. I was born at an alarming 8 pounds and 7 ounces. Tonio was smaller. He only weighed 7 pounds even. We were both born at Grady Memorial Hospital.

We lived in Decatur, Georgia. We had a three bedroom ranch-style house. It was nothing too fancy.

We were just your average middle-class dysfunctional family. Daddy had a good job. He worked as a foreman for General Motors. Mama cleaned various office buildings downtown.

She and my brother often went to church and bingo. Mama was young, so I never really understood why she went to bingo all the time. I'd always thought that it was for older people.

Mama told me that, when I was a baby, Daddy didn't care if I was asleep or awake, he'd come home

from work and hold me all day. Daddy really loved me and was so glad that he had a little girl.

My brother, Tonio, looked like Daddy. I looked like Mama's mother, but Mama never really talked about her mother. I don't know why. She just didn't. Mama was light-skinned with wavy hair. Daddy was tall, dark, and lovely. My hair wasn't wavy. I had to get a perm every three months or so. Tonio's hair was like Daddy's – nappy!

When I was about six, Daddy told me that I looked like a skinny Whitney Houston. As far as I could remember, I always knew that one day I was going to be a singer. I wanted to sing like Patti Labelle. The first time I saw her was on a music awards show. She sang her butt off.

I was Daddy's favorite, and Tonio was Mama's favorite. When we got out of school for the day, Tonio and I would fight over the remote control to the television. Whoever finished his or her homework first got to hog the television. I always finished before Tonio, but he'd always end up with the remote. Like I said, he was Mama's favorite. I didn't worry because, when Daddy got home from work, he'd make Tonio go into his and Mom's bedroom to watch television. Tonio didn't like to because they didn't have a color television.

I used to sit with Daddy on the sofa and watch my favorite cartoons. Daddy would tell me to go and get his pop. I would find out later that it was not pop at all. Well, it definitely was not the pop that I drank. Daddy and I would sit in the front room watching *Scooby Doo*. I always wanted to watch *The Smurfs*. Unfortunately, by the time Daddy got home, I could only watch *Scooby Doo*.

Daddy would turn that pop up while we watched cartoons. It was loud on his breath.

Mama would come in and say, "You know that stuff isn't good for you."

Daddy would say, "Yes, it is because I don't have to remember when I fuck you at night."

I don't know why Daddy was so mean to Mama, and I surely didn't know what the word "fuck" meant back then.

Mama would only say, "The food is in the oven. Tonio and I are going to bingo."

I used to sing for Daddy and his friends. Daddy had one friend that I loved very much. His name was Buck. Daddy had brothers and sisters, but they didn't come around much; so, Buck was more like a relative to Daddy. He would always tickle me until I had to use the restroom. I started calling him "Uncle Buck."

Daddy always had a party at our house every Saturday night. He would ask me to come in the front room to sing for him and his lions.

While Mama and Tonio were at bingo, Daddy's grown-up games had just begun…

Chapter Two
Daddy's Grown-Up Games

I remember the first time like it was yesterday. Mama and Tonio had gone to church and, after that, went straight to bingo. It was raining that Sunday morning. Daddy never went to church with them. Mama tried to wake me up, but Daddy said, "Leave her alone. Let her sleep."

Daddy told them to go on, have a good service, pray for him, and to also have a good night at bingo.

After Daddy saw them off, he came straight to my room. Daddy seemed taller and darker as he stood over me. He scared me!

"Are you awake, Tonae? Do you want some breakfast?"

"Yes, Daddy. I want some bacon, eggs, pancakes, and orange juice."

"Okay. Before we eat, we're going to play a grown-up game."

"A grown-up game?"

"Yes."

"It's called touch and feel."

"Okay, Daddy."

I had no idea what was about to happen. I was only six. What the hell did I know about a grown-up game?

Daddy continued, "Before we start, here are the rules. You can't tell anyone! I mean no one! You can't tell Mama or Tonio. You sure as hell can't tell that nosy ass pastor at the church."

"Okay, Daddy."

"Sit up in the bed."

"Now, remember, you can't tell anyone! If you do, I can't take you to McDonald's anymore," he warned.

As I stood up in the bed, Daddy stood tall in front of me. He had on a white t-shirt with his pajama pants. He took his shirt off and said, "Look at my chest. Do you know what these are?"

He pointed at his nipples.

"I want you to lick them."

I stood tall on my bed. Daddy's chest was right in my face. As I licked Daddy's nipples, his dick grew, poking me in my stomach. He laughed and said, "Look what you did."

"What did I do, Daddy?"

He pointed at his dick and said, "Now, you gotta touch it."

"Touch what?"

"My rod."

I timidly touched Daddy's long black you-know-what.

"Now, reach over there and get that baby oil. I want you to put it on my rod and jack it for me."

He smiled down at me.

"Good girl."

Then, he raised his head toward the ceiling.

"Yeah, keep doing it. Slow. Fast. Slow," he moaned.

I guess my pace wasn't good enough for Daddy because he grabbed his dick and told me to lie down on my back while he stood over me and jacked his rod

himself. Daddy started jerking, moaning loud, and calling my name. Finally, Daddy came all over my favorite Wonder Woman pajamas. I was in complete shock. I had just seen my daddy's rod throw up.

"Don't move. I'll clean it up. See how you made your daddy feel? You made me feel real good. I am so proud of you."

I laid there with my eyes closed. It had almost gotten in my face. Daddy got a washcloth and wiped it off. Smiling and looking at his watch, he said, "That game was fun. Did you like that game, Tonae?"

"Yes, Daddy."

I was ready to go to McDonald's. I didn't care about a stupid grown-up game with Daddy. As the years passed on, I grew used to Daddy and those stupid ass grown-up games.

"Maybe we can play another one before Mama and Tonio get back. Put some clothes on. Let's go to your favorite place—McDonald's."

I was so happy to go to McDonald's that I forgot to take off my favorite pajamas that Daddy's rod had thrown up on. I slipped my flower dress on over my pajamas and put on my mary janes. We got in his Volvo station wagon. I headed for the back seat.

"Get up here with me. I ain't gonna bite."

I reached for the seat belt.

He said, "Get in the middle. Sit right next to me. You don't gotta put on that seatbelt. I know how to drive."

He was driving with his left hand and had his right hand under my flower dress.

"How does that feel?

"It feels funny," I said.

"Spread your legs wider. Open them up!"

He pulled my panties to the side and slid his middle finger in my pooh-nanny.

"Now, how does that feel?"

"It hurts, Daddy."

While pinching me, he said, "It shouldn't hurt."

I even felt the cuts and crust on Daddy's big fingers. I wanted to jump through the windshield.

He said, "It's over now. We're at McDonald's."

When we walked in, I went straight to the bathroom. A white lady was in there with her daughter. The little girl and I were about the same age. We were both at the sink washing our hands. As they were leaving, the little girl said, "Mommy, that black girl stinks."

"That's not a nice thing to say, Sara," whispered the little girl's mother.

"But it's true, Mommy! That little black girl smells bad."

The lady looked at me and smiled. I didn't find shit funny. Now that I think back, she should have told her outspoken ass daughter to apologize. Instead, she said, "Sara, that's not a nice thing to say."

After drying my hands, I went crying to Daddy. He was already sitting down. He'd already ordered my favorite—the cheeseburger happy meal.

"Why are you crying?" Daddy asked.

"The little girl in the bathroom said I stink!"

"What!" My daddy said in disbelief. "Come here. Let me smell your neck."

As he reached over the table to get closer, he noticed my pajamas under my flower dress.

"Get up, Tonae. Let's go to the bathroom."

When we got in the bathroom, Daddy was very angry. He was mad because I had forgotten to take off my favorite pajamas.

"Why do you still have on those pajamas?"

"Daddy, these are my favorite Wonder Woman pajamas."

"That's where the smell is coming from."

Daddy's damp cum smelled loudly through my clothes.

"Take 'em off and give 'em to me. Do you know you could get me in trouble?"

"I'm sorry, Daddy."

He put my pajamas in his pocket. We grabbed our food and headed home.

When we got home, Daddy went to his room and grabbed a couple of his work pants. He put them in the washer along with my Wonder Woman pajamas. It was around 3 p.m. I asked Daddy if I could go outside.

He said, "No. Come in here and sit with me."

I sat there on the sofa with Daddy watching football. He reached under the sofa and grabbed his brown paper bag. He turned that Jack Daniels up and said, "You ready to play another game?"

"Sure, Daddy."

Luckily, I was saved by the bell. The doorbell rang, and it was Uncle Buck.

I asked Daddy to please let me go outside. I knew he would say yes 'cause Uncle Buck was there.

"Go on out there. Don't get lost. When you see your mama's car pull up, you get back in this house."

"Okay, Daddy."

Uncle Buck said, "Where you think you going, young lady? You know you gotta give your Uncle Buck some of that sweet sugar."

I ran and jumped in his arms. He kissed me on the cheek.

"She's gonna make some man a happy husband someday," Uncle Buck said.

I looked back and saw Daddy smiling with a wicked look on his face.

Uncle Buck asked Daddy to pass him some of that Jack Daniels. They continued to watch the football game.

Later that evening, after Uncle Buck had gone home, Tonio and Mama were eating in the kitchen. Mama spilled collard green juice and barbeque sauce from the rib plate she had gotten from church on her dress. She ran to take it off and put it in the washer so the stain wouldn't set. She looked in the washer and saw my pajama shirt in there with Daddy's work pants, but she didn't say one word. Mama knew right then and there that Daddy was molesting her only daughter...

Chapter Three
A Birthday to Remember

On my tenth birthday, I begged Mama to let me have a birthday party. My birthday fell on a Saturday. It seemed like every Saturday Mama and Daddy threw a party. She'd party Saturday nights. Then, she'd go to church on Sundays. Mama really didn't have a choice because, if she would have said no, Daddy would have overruled. Mama knew that Daddy and I had been intimate for the past four years now. I don't know why she never killed him for touching me. I had yet to find out. She always seemed somewhat distant and in her own world.

Neither Daddy nor Mama worked on weekends. Daddy and Uncle Buck were always in the living room drinking their favorite pop. They would listen to Johnny Taylor, Otis Redding, and Sam Cooke. I still listen to those oldies today.

Even though Mama knew what was going on between Daddy and me, she still tried to be a mother by buying my favorite cake. Mama had a big sheet cake made for me. She knew how much I loved Wonder Woman. The cake was red, white, and blue with the Wonder Woman emblem in the middle. We all gathered around the kitchen table.

Mama said, "I hope your wish comes true, Tonae."

"I hope so, too, Mama."

I wanted to tell Mama my wish, but I had heard that, if you tell your wish, it wouldn't come true.

Daddy said, "I know I'm gonna get the first slice."

The kind of slice I wanted to give Daddy was a slice from ear to ear. I cut Daddy a big piece with Wonder Woman's mask. Tonio asked if he could cut his own piece.

I said, "Nope. It's my birthday."

I cut him a very small piece. Daddy looked at Mama and said, "Where is the damn ice cream?"

Mama went out to get some ice cream. Daddy also told her to bring him a fifth of his favorite pop. Tonio tagged along. He was always with Mama.

Mama must have gotten tied up at the store because, while she was gone, I ate almost all of my cake. I was feeling sick. I went in my room to lie down.

Daddy had gotten tired of waiting for Mama to bring his favorite pop, so he asked Uncle Buck to keep an eye on me while he ran out to get it on his own.

Uncle Buck came in my room and turned on my Wonder Woman lamp, whispering my name as he did, "Tonae? Tonae? Are you 'sleep?"

"No. I'm just laying here, Uncle Buck. My tummy hurts."

"Your Uncle Buck is here. I can make that tummy ache go away. What do you want for your birthday? I'll get it when I get paid next Friday."

"Ooh, Uncle Buck, can you get me a Wonder Woman karaoke machine?"

"Yeah, I can get my little princess anything she wants. I can make your tummy feel better."

"How, Uncle Buck? You don't know any magic."

"Look and learn, little princess."

15

For some strange reason, I knew that Uncle Buck was going to play a grown-up game just like Daddy had been doing.

"Uncle Buck, you're not a magic man. You don't have special powers."

"Do you love your Uncle Buck?"

"Yes," I said, rubbing my stomach.

"Well, you have to trust your Uncle Buck. Let me listen to your stomach."

He laid his head on my stomach and listened, saying, "Yep, I know what it is."

"What is it, Uncle Buck?"

"You have to lay on your back, so I can massage the pain away. How does that feel?"

He gently massaged my stomach.

"It still hurts," I said, looking at him and seeing the horns grow from the top of his head.

He said, "Let's play a grown-up game. The name of this grown-up game is hospital."

He explained the rules just like Daddy had. He told me not to tell anyone, especially Daddy. He said that Daddy would kill him. Then, he wouldn't be able to buy me the Wonder Woman karaoke machine that I wanted for my birthday. He told me that he would be the doctor, and I would be the patient. He grabbed my hairbrush and, pretending that it was a stethoscope, listened to my heart. I just laid there, waiting for him to start touching me since Daddy had already done it so often. It didn't make a difference if my Uncle Buck did it, too. He pulled my shirt up and said, "You have little cherries up here on your chest."

He rubbed my nipples and asked me, "How does it feel?"

I told him that it felt weird.

Then, he licked them.

"Look at my pants. Do you know what that is sticking   out?

"No," I lied.

I had seen Daddy's rod plenty of times. He pulled his rod out, and it was two tones— black and pink.

It wasn't big like Daddy's. It was short and fat.

He said, "Touch it."

I touched it, and it was semi-hard.

"If I wasn't an old man, I'd marry you."

Uncle Buck was older than Daddy. I think by fifteen years.

I said, "For real, Uncle Buck? You'd marry me?"

"Yep. I sure would, and I'd buy you all the Wonder Woman stuff you wanted. Get that hair grease, put it on my rod, and play with it."

I was familiar with this. Daddy had made me do this numerous times.

"Girl, if I didn't know better, I'd think you'd done this before. You wanna taste it? Just joking. Keep stroking."

I don't think he was joking.

"I'm almost there."

I knew he was getting ready to let go. It didn't take him long when I was jacking his dick. He was looking at the ceiling, saying, "Yeah, Diane Carroll, suck this dick. Don't be selfish. Give Lena Horne some. Lena, share this dick. Let Dorothy Dandridge finish me off."

I didn't have to worry about Uncle Buck's cum getting on me because his dick was too small. It got all over his shoes.

He said, "Good girl, Tonae. I'll have that karaoke machine for you next week. Remember to keep this a secret. If you don't, I won't be able to get that karaoke machine for you."

17

"Okay, Uncle Buck."

When it was all over, my stomach hurt even worse. I hated having to look at Uncle Buck's shriveled up dick. He went back to the living room and acted like nothing ever happened. I just laid there thinking that, if I kept being good to Daddy and Uncle Buck, I could get all the McDonald's and Wonder Woman stuff I wanted.

Daddy and Mama pulled up at the same time. Daddy came in fussing, talking about how he had missed the football game. It was Saturday. That football shit came on Sundays. What he meant was he missed out on our grown-up game, but Uncle Buck had beat him to it that time.

Tonio ran in my room, yelling, "Get up, Tonae. It's still your birthday."

I didn't want to get up. My stomach was still hurting from eating all that damn cake.

"Well, since you're not gonna get up, can I ride your Wonder Woman bike?"

I kept telling Tonio my bike was for a girl, but Tonio didn't care. It seemed that he felt something was wrong with me. He continued to beg to ride my bike, and I finally said, "Go ahead, Tonio. Help yourself."

Chapter Four
Tonio's 9th Birthday Party

One year later, it was Tonio's 9th birthday. He got a Super Nintendo and was allowed to let one boy spend the night. I begged Tonio to let it be Bobby Knight. Bobby had moved into our neighborhood the summer before. I remember because I had started my period that summer. Tonio thought that he was Wesley Snipes, and Bobby thought he was G Money. They really thought they were the Cash Money Brothers that night. I really liked Bobby, too. When he used to walk to the candy lady, I would give him one dollar to buy himself a Kool-Aid freeze.

That night I planned to sneak into Tonio's room, so I could get Bobby to notice me. I mean he played with me outside, but I wanted to jack his dick like I had done Daddy and Uncle Buck. I wanted to have him moaning my name just like Daddy did. I didn't have to worry about Daddy coming in my room that night and playing grown-up games because we had company over. Sometimes that still didn't stop Daddy. He'd tell Mama that he was going on the porch to smoke a cigarette and would come in my room. Most nights, I just prepared myself for Daddy. I would lay in the bed naked and wait.

I was in my room, contemplating how I could get Bobby hooked. I put on the smallest shorts I could find.

Daddy said I looked like Whitney Houston, and that night was my time to find out. I wanted to see if Bobby would think the same thing.

Bobby was in Tonio's room and all into that video game. I walked in and said, "Boy, when you come in my house, you speak to the lady of the house."

"The lady of the house is sleep, and you don't pay any bills," Bobby said.

Technically, I was the lady of the house because, by then, I was sucking Daddy's dick almost three times a week.

I knocked the controller out of his hand. He picked it back up without even noticing my long legs or my shiny, wet lips. I went back to my room wondering what it would be like to jack Bobby's dick.

I was in my mirror singing Patti "I Got a New Attitude." My door was cracked, and I saw Bobby's head peaking in. He said, "Girl, you can't sing."

I had a feeling that he liked me, too.

I said, "Boy, I'm going to be a famous singer one day."

I waited until it was very late. I didn't have to worry about Tonio waking up because he slept like a bear during winter. When they both were sound asleep, I crept into the room. Tonio was asleep on the bed with the controller still in his hand. Bobby was asleep on Tonio's big yellow bean bag with the controller still in his hand. Daddy used to tell me to get his dick hard first. After it was hard, I would massage it. First, slow; then, fast. Daddy used to love for me to use baby oil. Well, that night, shampoo was going to have to work because I didn't have anymore baby oil. I rubbed the outside of Bobby's pants; sure enough, his rod got hard, but it wasn't big. Anyway, I unzipped his pants and pulled his dick out of the zipper part of his pants. He was sleeping

hard until he felt that cold shampoo on his dick. He opened up his eyes and screamed, "Girl, what the fuck are you doing?"

I said, "Bobby, I'm trying to make you feel good."

He said, "How? By putting shampoo on my dick?"

Lather was everywhere. I was so embarrassed. I went in my room and fell asleep. The next morning, neither one of us spoke about the shampoo incident.

Chapter Five
Daddy Ain't No Saint

When I was twelve years old, Daddy would always play them grown-up games when Mama and Tonio were at church and bingo. Daddy would come in my room every Sunday morning.

"Daddy, why can't I go to church with Mama and Tonio?"

"Why do you wanna go to church when you got your daddy?"

I had been praying that Daddy would die for years. Every birthday, it was the same wish. I just wanted Daddy to drop dead. I figured, if I went to church, God would hear me better.

Daddy said, "You don't need to go to church. We have to play our grown-up game, remember?"

"Yes, Daddy."

"Now, Tonae, you're getting older, so I'm going to explain the rules again. This game will be more fun. First rule: Don't tell Mama or Tonio. Second rule: Always do as I say. Third rule: Don't make Daddy mad. Fourth rule: Do not tell that nosy ass Pastor Riley."

"Okay, Daddy."

"Oh, yeah. You can't even tell God!"

Even I knew God was watching Daddy's every move. If Daddy would have gone to church with Mama,

he would have known that God saw everything. Everything!

"Tonae, you know you are developing into a nice young lady."

"Yes, Daddy, I know."

"You remember all them times you jacked my rod?"

"Yes, Daddy."

"Well, this time you're gonna feel my rod."

Daddy turned up his favorite pop and said, "Do you know about the birds and the bees?"

"A little, Daddy. I know I can have a baby."

When I said the word "baby", Daddy frowned and started to ask about me and Bobby.

"I see how you look at Bobby. What all you and that boy done?"

"Daddy, Bobby is only a boy I have a crush on. I have only kissed him on the cheek," I lied.

Daddy turned his brown paper bag up and said, "Let the games begin. Come on in our room. I'll play Bobby and you'll play Mama."

"Why do I have to play Mama? Why can't I play Patti LaBelle?"

"Because your mama was the tender age you are now when I first had her. Since you're twelve now, I want you to feel how Mama felt. Plus I want you to take me years back to when I first met your mama."

This shit didn't make any sense to me, but Daddy insisted that, if I kept our sexual encounters to myself, I would get whatever I wanted. I felt nervous being in their room. Mama didn't allow anyone in her room. No church people. No insurance man. No one! Mama was a real neat freak. They had a king size bed with cherry wood bedroom furniture. I was so nervous that I bumped into the dresser and knocked over their

wedding picture. Daddy looked like he could have been Mama's daddy in that picture. You would think that would have fazed him, but not my daddy, not one bit.

I sat in his chair.

He said, "Get your ass in the bed."

"Mama will kill me," I said, knowing she didn't care. She had allowed Daddy to touch me for six years now.

"You let me worry about her. Besides, you are her today in this game. We'll make it back up later. Go in there, and get your mama's lingerie. Put on those red pumps, too."

Mama's feet and mine were practically the same size. I put them on. This was what Mama must have worn for Daddy when she was twelve for real because the lingerie fit me to a tee.

"Now, walk like them supermodels on TV."

I had never seen any supermodels on TV. So, I walked like Smurfette. She was a cute blonde.

"Okay, Daddy."

I was ready to get this over with. I wanted to go to church, so God could hear me loud and clear because on my next birthday I wanted Daddy to be dead.

"I'm not Daddy. I'm Bobby, remember?"

"Okay, Bobby."

Daddy really had a problem. Daddy was the devil himself. He didn't care about the tears I had in my eyes while he was fucking me. He didn't care about whether or not he got me pregnant. All he cared about was getting his dick sucked and catching a fat ass nut in my ass or my mouth.

"This is just a game. Don't spoil it, okay?" Daddy continued.

"Okay, Daddy—I mean Bobby."

"Are you ready to feel what Mama felt at twelve?"

"Yes, Daddy—I mean Bobby."

"That's enough walking. Take it off and get in the bed. Are you nervous?"

"Yes, Daddy—I mean Bobby."

He was sitting in his chair and rubbing his dick. I was completely naked.

"Get over here."

I stood in front of Daddy, watching him turn up his friend, Jack.

"Turn around," he said, looking like a perverted child molester.

"You look just like Mama did. Bend over."

I bent over and when I turned to face him, I had tears in my eyes.

"What's wrong? Don't cry. This will be fun. I promise. I'm Bobby, remember? Here. Drink some of this. This will help."

I turned it up just like I had seen Daddy do. I almost threw up on the both of us.

"Amateur! Run into the kitchen and get some Coke and ice."

I reached for Mama's housecoat that was on the ottoman.

Daddy said, "You don't need that. Go. Run naked. I wanna see your body shake."

When I got back, Daddy was already in the bed. He had taken his shirt off. He had on his boxer drawers. He mixed my drink. Not only was I about to fuck my daddy, I was also going to drink with him.

"Now, how does that taste?"

"Still nasty."

He added a little more Coke.

"Now, how is that?" he asked, rubbing his chest.

I drank it all up in one gulp. I wanted to get drunk and not remember fucking him just like he had told Mama. He was still drinking it like water.

"Get in the bed," Daddy commanded.

Once I got in the bed, I just sat there and stared at their wedding picture.

"Bobby, can you lay that picture on the dresser down?"

"You called me Bobby. Now, you're getting into the game."

Daddy got up and laid the picture down.

"We're going to watch a movie. I want you to do everything you see them do in the movie to me."

It was a nasty porn flick. The stars were a tall white man with black hair and two blonde chicks. That man had the biggest dick anyone could possibly have.

"Look. You see that, Tonae?"

I had covered my eyes with my fingers. I peaked through them.

"Don't be shy. I'm Bobby, remember?"

"Okay, Daddy—I mean Bobby."

Daddy started to take his boxers off. He was wrinkled almost on his everything. I kept watching the tape. It blew my mind. The man was jacking his dick while the ladies were eating each other out, but watching Daddy's big black uncircumcised dick blew me even more. I looked back at the movie. The ladies were taking turns slurping on the man's dick. His dick was so big. They could suck it together. They were on a balcony on a mat by an Olympic size pool.

"That's what I want you to do to me," Daddy said, grinning ear to ear.

"What, Bobby?"

"Clean this shit up good. Don't miss one spot. Clean this shit up and try again."

I cleaned it up.

"Look, Daddy. Look at what they're doing now."

They were jacking his dick.

"Yeah, do that because you are pissing me off. Can't even suck your own daddy's dick. Go get the baby oil. You still remember how to do that, don't you?"

"Yes, Daddy — I mean Bobby."

"When I cum, I want you to catch it with your mouth. That nice man on TV got them ladies that nice house with that pool. Don't you want all those nice things?"

"Yes, Daddy — I mean Bobby."

"You gotta do what I ask you to do and not make me mad."

He was getting ready to let go because he was jacking it real fast, and — Swoosh! — Daddy exploded in my mouth.

"That's a good girl. Swallow it! Swallow it," Daddy screamed.

It was slimy, thick, and nasty sliding down my throat. Daddy continued to drink his pop. I went to my room to change clothes. Daddy was asleep thirty minutes later. I went outside to play with the real Bobby Knight...

Chapter Six
Daddy, Please Play with My Brother, Tonio

When I was fourteen years old, Tonio was thirteen. We both were excited about going to middle school. Tonio kept good grades, so he had no problem getting on the school's junior basketball team. When we got home, Mama was in the kitchen as usual. She was cooking smothered cubed steak, gravy over rice, string beans and cornbread. Even though we lived in the city part of Georgia, we hardly ever ate out as a family. Only Daddy and I did. When we went out to eat, Mama would get pissed because we didn't eat her cooking.

"Mama, you got it smelling good up in here," I said.

"Yeah, Mama, you put your foot in the food," Tonio said.

Mama was at the table, writing in a notebook. Tonio and I sat at the table in the front room. We no longer argued over who got the remote first because he was excited about basketball and I was too busy trying to get Bobby Knight to notice me even more. Even though I was rocking the hottest fashions, I still wanted to suck his dick like I did Daddy's. Bobby had gotten taller. He looked even better in the 8th grade. He and Tonio were the same age. I used to write him love notes in school asking him to skip gym class. I wanted him to meet me

in the old burned out building that used to be the gym. I remember the first time he came.

"Let me see that rod, Bobby."

"See what?" He asked, acting like he didn't know what I was talking about.

"You know what. That dick."

"Girl, what do you know about a damn rod?"

"I bet I can suck it like a pro."

I had plenty of experience. Thanks to Daddy and Uncle Buck. Sucking Bobby's dick would be a piece of cake.

"What? You wanna put my dick in your mouth?"

"Yeah, and I don't got any shampoo around."

We both smiled.

"Now, get over here and whip it out."

The gym still smelled like burnt wood, but I didn't worry about that. This was my chance to hook Bobby.

"Girl, your daddy will kill me if he finds out I let you suck my dick."

I thought, *My daddy ain't going to do shit because I suck his dick at least three times a week.*

"I make my daddy happy. That's how I kick the latest and newest clothes. Quit wasting time, Bobby. We gotta get back to class."

"Well, hurry up 'cause I don't like being in this old scary building," Bobby said.

"What? The basketball captain is scared?"

"Tonae, just hurry."

"Boy, shut your whining and put your dick in my mouth."

I couldn't believe it. Bobby's dick was skinny like a pencil. I had no problem deep throating that skinny ass dick. It was perfect. It didn't fill my mouth like Daddy's and Uncle Buck's dicks. I sucked his dick both fast and

slow. Then, I took it out of my mouth and licked down the shaft. When I looked up at him, he had his notebook over his face and was making real ugly face expressions.

"Wait. Stop. I gotta pee," he said, snatching his dick out my mouth.

"No, you don't have to pee, boy. You're about to cum."

"I'm about to what?"

"You never had sperm to come out your dick?"

"No, I haven't. And how do you know so much about my dick anyway?"

I was only fourteen, but I knew more about his dick than he did.

"Whatever. Hold on a minute. I gotta pee," he said.

He went to the corner to try to pee, but nothing came out.

"I told you, fool. Now, I gotta start over. Don't fight the feeling, Bobby. Just let it go in my mouth. Bobby, just concentrate. When you feel like you have to pee again, just let your body go. Think about Janet Jackson or Shelia E. Hell! Think about Patti Labelle."

"That old ass lady?"

"That old ass lady is rich, and I'm gonna be a rich singer like her someday."

"I'll think of you as Penny on *Good Times*, sucking my dick."

"Duh, I said Janet Jackson."

"Oh, yeah. That is her, isn't it?" he said, smiling and enjoying me sucking his dick.

This boy had no clue. If I was going to be rich and famous one day, I wanted his fine ass by my side.

"Damn, Penny, you sucking this dick like dynamite!!!!! I gotta pee."

"No, you don't. Let it go, Bobby."

I was charmed by his humor. I sucked his dick so good. When he finally came, I swallowed every drop just like Daddy had taught me to do.

"Penny—I mean Tonae, you swallowed that shit? Who else's dick you been sucking? I haven't seen you around school with anyone else."

I thought, *Boy, you see me with my daddy all the time. You don't have the slightest idea that it is my daddy's dick that I've been sucking.*

No one would ever think that I became a dick-sucking pro by sucking my own daddy's dick. Bobby went back to class. When I got home, Mama was in the kitchen, sitting at the table and writing in her notebook.

"What you writing, Mama?"

"I'm adding up bills," Mama said, rolling her eyes.

It didn't look like math to me. She was writing something. Daddy got home with his cooler in one hand and his brown bag in the other.

"Daddy, I want to play basketball," Tonio said, "Mama already said yes. I just need you to take me to the gym to practice my jump shot."

"I work almost one hundred hours a week," Daddy said, "Your mama hardly works. She'll take you."

"Today is Wednesday, isn't it?" Mama said, looking at me, "Tonio, get ready. Maybe we can still catch bingo. It's still early. Tonae, the food is in the oven. Take care of your daddy 'til I get back."

I had been taking care of Daddy for almost seven years now.

"Bye, Tonio. Remember I'm going to be the singer and you're going to be the NBA player."

I loved my brother, and I knew he loved me. It really hurt him that Daddy wasn't the one taking him to the gym.

"One of y'all needs to be a fucking doctor because I'm getting old," Daddy said.

"If I was a doctor, I'd let your ass die," I said under my breath.

Mama said, "Come on, Tonio. We can stop by the gym for an hour, and I can still catch bingo."

"Yeah, y'all got plenty of time," Daddy said.

I knew what Daddy was thinking. He was ready to play another grown-up game. My heart was screaming, "Daddy, please play with Tonio!"

Chapter Seven
Mama, I Want to Sing

I wanted to be a singer so bad that I could taste it. Our school had an upcoming talent show. I just knew I would win it because I had been singing for my daddy and his friends since I was six years old. I used to stand in the front room while Daddy and Uncle Buck drank his favorite pop. Daddy used to say, "Tonae, come in here and show these two old goats how you can sing like Patti."

I would sing "Lady Marmalade."

"Hurry up. Show this fool that you're going to be famous one day," Daddy said, pointing at Uncle Buck.

"Yeah, don't forget your Uncle Buck when you get rich and famous," Uncle Buck said.

Yeah, I'm going to forget about your ass just like you forgot about my Wonder Woman karaoke machine, I thought. Once I finished singing, I went and sat on Daddy's lap. I had on my blue jean Levi's skirt, a pink turtleneck, my white tights, and a pair of mary janes. When Uncle Buck went to the bathroom, Daddy put his hand under my skirt.

"Damn. How many clothes do you have on?"

Daddy reached in his pants, took out his pocket knife, and cut the crotch of my tights. He then put one of his dirty crusty finger in my vagina. No matter how many times Daddy fingered me, I never got used to it.

34

"You like that?"

"No," I said.

"You'll like it soon," he said as Uncle Buck walked back into the room.

I couldn't wait to get home and tell Mama about the talent show.

"Mama, can you please get me the same dress that Patti had on when she performed on the music awards?"

"Go ask Daddy. You ask him for everything else."

All this was her fault in the first place. I never understood why Mama just didn't buy a gun and shoot Daddy. Maybe she was just as sick as he was. She was sitting in the kitchen. No food was cooking. She was at the table adding up bills in her notebook. I had to get that notebook and see what Mama was writing in there.

"Sure, Mama. I'll ask Daddy. What are you writing?"

"Tonae, why are you so damn nosy?"

"I'm not nosy, Mama. I just wanted to know if you were writing to God or something. We keep a journal at school, and we usually have to write about how our day went."

Mama looked at me with tears in her eyes.

"Tonae, I stopped believing in God a long time ago."

I didn't know what Mama meant, so I said, "Isn't God at church? And you go there all the time."

"Tonae, I do that because I'm tired of looking at your daddy."

I kissed Mama on the cheek and went to talk on the phone until Daddy got home from work. Mama had

gotten Tonio a basketball goal. He was outside shooting hoops. I had the phone all to myself, so I called Bobby.

"Hello."

"What's up, Bobby?'

"Who dis?"

"This is your favorite dick sucker."

"Oh, hold on." He clicked over and came back.

"Who was that on the other line, Bobby?"

"Oh, that wasn't nobody but Shelia Jones."

"Shelia who?"

I had been sucking his dick faithfully for almost a year now.

"What is she to you? Is she sucking your dick, too?"

"No, she's doing better. She's giving up the pussy."

She was head of the cheerleader squad, but I didn't care.

I said, "I can suck and fuck. Where is your mama? I can come and show you what I can do now."

I didn't have to worry about Bobby's daddy because he was locked up for selling drugs.

"My mama is gone."

Daddy wasn't going to get home until another hour. That was more than enough time for me to do what I had to do.

"I'll see you in a minute."

I hung up and flew out the door. I lied to Mama and told her I was going outside to shoot hoops with Tonio. I ran down to Bobby's house. When I got there, he was still on the phone. It must have been Shelia Jones because he lied and said, "Hey, I gotta call you back. My mama wants me." Then to me, he said, "Now, what's that shit you was talking? You ain't gave up the pussy yet?"

"Boy, I can suck you; then, fuck you. I'm a pro."

We took our clothes off, and I got on my knees. Bobby had a white ring around his dick.

"What's that white stuff?"

"Probably powder or something."

"Oh, okay."

I put his dick in my mouth. Not only was it salty, but it had an odor.

"Do you got some mouthwash?" I asked with that sour ass taste in my mouth.

"Man, are you gonna suck this dick or not?"

He was looking good as ever. I got up, put the mouthwash in my mouth, and swished it around in my mouth a couple of times. I got back down on my knees to suck his dick. He already had pre-cum leaking out. At least, that's what I thought it was.

I said, "Just chill out. Don't rush perfection."

Because I had that mint taste in my mouth, I could barely taste the residue he had on his dick.

"Don't suck it 'til I cum. Remember you said you're gonna suck and fuck."

I jumped on his dick and rode him like I had seen them ladies do on that porn I used to watch with Daddy. He pushed me off right before he came.

"I'm not getting your ass pregnant."

I caught every drop that squirted out and swallowed it. That wasn't the only thing I caught. Two days later, my throat was swollen. Mama took me to the doctor. He gave me some medication. It was cleared up in three days. I didn't tell anyone I had gotten an infection. Not even Bobby.

Chapter Eight
Talent Show Showdown

When I walked back in the house from fucking and sucking Bobby, Daddy was pulling up into the driveway. Although I hated fucking and sucking Daddy, I loved it because he got me whatever I asked for. That didn't make sense back then, and it don't make sense now.

I had to ask as soon as he walked in the door. I knew that, if I didn't ask right then, he would start drinking, and Daddy didn't drink and drive.

"Daddy, can you please take me to Kessler's so I can get the dress that Patti LaBelle had on at the music awards? We have a talent show tomorrow, and I want to look good."

"That dress probably costs a million dollars," Daddy said, scratching his head, "You caught me right before I started drinking."

"Let's go. We'll find a dress close to it."

As we left, I saw Mama peeking around the corner. When we got to the car, Tonio came flying around the corner. He asked Daddy if he could go with us.

"No, you can't because we are going shopping for girl stuff."

Tonio's feelings were hurt. He bounced the ball and continued to shoot hoops. I knew Tonio wished we

could change spots. I knew he wanted Daddy to do more stuff with him. When we got in the car, Daddy didn't waste no time unzipping his pants. He said, "You can suck my dick on the way to get the dress you want."

If I didn't know any better, he was fucking the same person Bobby was fucking. He had a white ring around his dick, too. I smelled his aroma. It smelled like Shower to Shower body powder.

I said, "Okay." And put Daddy's dick in my mouth.

Daddy said, "Don't suck it until I cum. I want to get some of that tight pussy."

This was the first time Daddy would have actually fucked me. We'd always played stupid games. Daddy told me to get on his dick. I couldn't because the steering wheel was in the way. When that didn't work, he pulled into the dark parking lot of an old store that was being remodeled. He told me to get outside and bend over. I was afraid of being outside. He said, "Girl, ain't nobody out here. Bend over."

I bent over and spread my ass all the way open. I was ready to go get my Patti dress. Daddy put his dick in me. It didn't hurt because Bobby was the first person I ever had intercourse with. Daddy didn't know that.

He said, "Your pussy isn't tight like I thought it would be. Have you been fucking that damn Bobby boy?"

"No, Daddy. You know I'm your little angel."

He grabbed my hair and fucked me hard, like we were making a porn movie. He was fucking me and saying, "Tonae, I don't know what I'll do if another man comes near you."

I can't lie. His dick felt better than Bobby's. I took all of Daddy's dick. He filled my pussy all the way up. When Daddy came, he didn't come out like Bobby

39

did. He came all up in my pussy. When it was over, he grabbed me, turned me around, and kissed me. His kiss was cold as death.

He said, "You have to promise to let me be the only man for you."

"Yes, Daddy. Whatever you say."

We got my dress and all the accessories to match. When we got home, Tonio was in his room, and Mama was in the kitchen, writing in her notebook. I went in the room to practice my singing and dance moves for the talent show. After I got out of the shower, I went to eat a bowl of cereal. Mama was asleep on the sofa in the living room. I tried calling Bobby but got no answer. The next morning, I couldn't wait to get dressed. I wanted Mama to see how good I looked in my dress, but she had already gone to work. I was in the mirror curling my hair when Tonio came in, saying, "Girl, why are you wearing that now? The talent show isn't until after school."

"I know when the talent show is. I want to look good all day. Besides, I have to out do this Shelia chick. Bobby said whoever wins the talent show will be the one he takes to the prom."

"Shelia." Tonio said her name like he knew her.

"Yes," I said giving him an evil look, "Shelia Jones. Do you know her?"

"Yes. I know her. She's with Bobby at practice almost everyday."

"Bobby told me that he was tutoring after school."

I knew he was fucking someone else because he told me, but I didn't know that he was going with her.

"Hurry up. I have to brush my teeth," Tonio said.

I told him to go to Mama's bathroom, and he said no because she would kill him. I said, "Who's going to tell? Are you going to tell on yourself?"

He looked confused and went in their room. I wasn't mad because Bobby was fucking someone else. I was mad because that bitch had been hanging around him at practice. I used to ask him if I could watch him practice, but he told me that he had tutoring. If he had tutoring, he wouldn't have been on the basketball team. I looked at myself in the mirror, put on a dab of fuchsia lipstick, and blew myself a kiss. That was my day. Fuck Shelia Jones. When I got to the bus stop, all the kids whispered and looked at me like I was crazy.

Tonio said, "I told you not to wear that dress."

"Shut up. Those kids are just jealous."

I didn't go to first period. Instead, Bobby and I went to our meeting place and fucked like rabbits. I went to my 2nd period class. I didn't like Ms. Lawrence. She would always ask me where I got my clothes from. When I walked in, she said, "Look, class. We have a new student. Oh, no, we don't. That's Miss Tonae."

I didn't find that shit funny. I wanted to go through the day without getting anything on my Patti dress. I saw Ms. Lawrence looking at me under those glasses, pretending to teach. When class was over, Ms. Lawrence asked to speak with me. She wanted to be nosy and ask me where I got such an expensive dress from. I told her that my daddy had bought it for me. She then asked me, "What kind of work does your daddy do?"

I told her, "Since I am a good girl, Daddy gives me whatever I want."

"Is that right?" she said, looking down at me with those ugly eyeglasses. I walked out with my head held high. If she had fucked her daddy like I did, she would have gotten nice shit, too. It was almost lunchtime. I had done good. I didn't get a pencil or pen mark on my Patti dress. I went to the cafeteria. Pizza was on the menu. I

41

ate my pizza and took two sips of my chocolate milk. I was good until, all of a sudden, this girl came out of nowhere and bumped into me, dropping her pizza all over my dress.

"Oops," she said, laughing as she walked by.

I said, "Excuse you, bitch."

She said, "No. Excuse you, dick sucker."

The whole cafeteria got quiet. I knew that was Shelia Jones, but she didn't look how I had pictured her. She was short with curly hair. She kind of looked like Paula Abdul. As soon as I was about to stab her with my fork, the security guard grabbed my hand and escorted us both to the office. The principal was out, so we had to talk to the counselor, Mrs. Vaughn. She gave us a warning because of the talent show. We were the two out of three that would be competing. If we had gotten suspended, there wouldn't have been a talent show. I was in shock. Not only did she fuck up my Patti dress, she had also called me a dick sucker in front of everyone. I was just standing there with tears in my eyes, but it was not because I was sad. I was mad because I couldn't stab her for fucking up my dress. I didn't worry about the stain because I knew how to sing and move like Patti. I left wondering what she was going to sing or if she knew how to sing. She told the counselor that she was sick, and she called her mom to come and get her. Since she went home, that automatically eliminated her ass from the talent show. I knew for sure Bobby would take me to the prom. The talent show was held in the auditorium. Mama and Daddy weren't there, but Tonio was there to watch me sing my heart out. I had a voice, and I was going to let the whole school hear it. I was hoping that a big shot music producer would be there, but it was only students, faculty, and Mr. Gomez, a janitor who had been there for almost twenty years. According to the ballot,

we were going on stage in alphabetical order. Mr. Kimes called the first contestants. They were the twins, Sasha and Rasha Henderson.

They both stood up and, at the same time and said, "We're present."

Then, he called Shelia Jones.

I proudly stood up and said, "She's not here."

"Speak for yourself," she said, waltzing in there in the same dress that I had on.

I was so pissed off. She had faked like she was sick so she could get her mom to buy her the exact same dress as mine.

The twins went first. They rapped "Brass Monkey," a song by the Beastie Boys. They had on Kangols, black and white Adidas suits, and matching black and white shell toe Adidas. They were white girls with flavor. They did good, but there were only two of them. The Beastie Boys were a trio group. When they were done, they got a cheer from the crowd. Nothing major, but they did okay. The next one to go was Shelia Jones. She looked pretty. She looked like one of them girls that were on Daddy's porn. She was my rival. She took my boyfriend, fucked up my Patti dress, called me a dick sucker in front of the whole school, and there I was having sexual feelings for her. She walked up there all slow, like she was making an entrance at the Academy Awards. The song she chose was called "All Cried Out," by Lisa Lisa. She sang it to Bobby. I saw her constantly watching him. He was in the 3rd row. I was heated on the inside. What made matters worse, she was thicker than me, so she filled that dress up with every inch of her body. I closed my eyes and imagined her singing to me. I pictured her wearing a black two piece bikini with the nipples and ass cut out. I was licking on her pecan colored nipples. My pussy got wet. I couldn't believe I

43

was thinking about her in that way after all she'd done to me. She was looking good, too. *What's wrong with me? Am I gay?* She was on the stage for three minutes; but, to me, my fantasy lasted every bit of twenty minutes.

"Tonae Watson! Tonae Watson!"

I was in a daze, imagining myself eating Shelia's pussy just like them ladies I had seen in Daddy's porn. I finally snapped out of it and went on stage. Shelia looked at me, rolled her eyes, and sat right next to Bobby. I forgot all about my ruined dress. I began to sing Patti "Lady Marmalade." I only took a short glimpse at Bobby and acted like I was the real Patti. I acted like I was at the music awards. I walked across the stage and gave every section eye contact. I blew that song. I had all eyes on me. Almost at the end of the song, I heard Tonio say, "That's my sister. She can blow!"

When I heard the word blow, all I could think about was all the dicks I had sucked. Daddy's, Uncle Buck's, and Bobby's. When I looked at Shelia, those memories went away. *That was it! I had to have her! I had to have Shelia!* I was tired of fucking Daddy. I wanted someone I could love and someone who would love me back. The only thing I wanted deep down inside was to be with a girl. Mama hardly showed me any love at all. Tonio showed brotherly love, and Daddy showed the wrong kind of love. Period. I had to admit that, after watching all that porn with Daddy, I did like the girl on girl action more.

Not only did I get the loudest cheer, I got a standing ovation. I won the talent show. We all had to show good sportsmanship by shaking each others' hands afterward. We didn't get a prize. It was just an event our school had because of our good behavior. The twins cried because they didn't win. It was only a talent show, but their whole family showed up. It was like they were

auditioning for a music contract. When it was time for Shelia and I to shake hands, I felt a feeling I couldn't describe when I touched her hand. We made eye contact, and my pussy got moist again. Looking at her and being that close to her made my clit jump. I felt a connection to her. I just didn't know how to tell her, and I wondered if she felt the same way.

Chapter Nine
Prom Time

It was hot on the day of the prom. I looked like Whitney Houston. Well, at least that's what Daddy told me. I wanted my long pretty legs to show. My daddy took me to Rich's and let me pick out whatever I wanted because I had fucked him good the night before. I picked out a black Guess body dress with a pair of Nine West pumps with some gold earrings and a gold purse to match. Bobby kept his word about taking me to the prom since I had won the talent show. I won, but that still didn't stop him from fucking Shelia. His mama was gonna drop us off. When it was time to go, he came to my door looking like DJ Quik. He had on a red nylon shirt, a pair of Jordache jeans, and a pair of Stan Smith's.

"Why aren't you dressed?" I asked, trying to keep my cool.

"I am dressed,' he said, rubbing his chin. "I'm wearing this."

"Boy, you look like a wanna be player."

"I am a player."

"Speaking of player. How did that bitch Shelia know I was dick sucker?"

I felt bad for calling her a bitch. I didn't know why. I just did.

"Man, don't believe that shit. Okay? I told her that you suck my dick better than she does, and she fucks me better than you do."

I couldn't believe what I was hearing. Bobby had told her all our secrets.

"Does she know about our hideaway at the old burned down gym?"

"Yes. We go there, too."

I felt so betrayed. I told Bobby I didn't want to go to the prom. I went in the house to change clothes. He walked away, smiling like he didn't care. I put on my sweatsuit and joined Tonio outside, who was playing a game of 21. Tonio really knew how to handle that ball. Tonio's dream was to be a professional basketball player, and I was going to be a famous singer. Tonio really didn't have a girlfriend in school. He wasn't really into girls. He just stayed focused, kept up his grades, and continued to play basketball for our school. I tried to block a shot, and it went in the street. As I ran after the ball, Bobby's mother's car stopped in front of me. I looked up and saw Bobby and Shelia in the backseat. They were on their way to the prom. It didn't matter to Bobby that he had two girls. He didn't care as long as he was having sex with us both. That's how I got that infection in my throat. He was fucking both of us with no protection. I wanted to stop Bobby's mother's car and snatch him out, but I played it off cool. I ran back to my yard, gave Tonio the ball, and went in my room. I made a promise not to give myself to Bobby anymore.

Chapter Ten
Mama's Pain

I knew that Mama wasn't adding up bills in that notebook for all those years. When I found the notebook, I saw that she had been keeping a journal, and it was dated back to her childhood. Mama and I never really talked about her mother. She had told me that she was dead.

I had once asked, "Mama, how did she die?"

She said, "She just did. Okay!"

Mama didn't want to talk about her mother. I was fine with it until I found her notebook. It had been a while since I had seen Bobby or Shelia around school. I was in the tenth grade then. One day, I was in the kitchen about to read Mama's notebook, while Tonio was playing basketball. Daddy was at work. I don't know where Mama was at, maybe at work, too. I had privacy. Tonio was in eye view, playing hoops. I could see him from the kitchen. I opened up Mama's notebook and it read:

June 10, 1970

I'm trying to sleep, and Mama is in there playing loud music with those blue lights flashing. If I had a door, it wouldn't be so bad. The music is so loud. I can't go back to sleep. Mama got into it with one of her drunk friends one

night, and my bedroom door has been off the hinges ever since. I can see Mama laid out in the hallway. One of Mama's friends is leaning over her. His name is Antonio. He's her live-in boyfriend. He isn't my daddy. Mama told me that my daddy was dead. Mama was in and out of consciousness. Earlier, Antonio had rolled up her sleeve and put what appeared to be a thick rubber band around her arm. Then, he grabbed a needle, thumped it, and stuck it in her arm. She just smiled at him and said, "I love you. One day, we're going to get married and have kids of our own. I love you so much."

Then, she passed out. He just laughed and said, "This will be your last fix for a while. You have to get back out there and make some money."

Mama told me that she worked as a night clerk at a hotel. She'd come home with lots of money and give it to her boyfriend, Antonio. I wanted to go to the bathroom earlier. Just when I thought the coast was clear, Mama's boyfriend, Antonio, was in the bathroom with the door open. He turned around and said, "Look who's awake. Nay Nay, you sure are looking more and more like your mother each day."

He zipped his pants up and told me to come on in and use the bathroom. At first, I wasn't going in there with him. Then, he said, "Are you afraid of me? You don't have nothing I've never seen before."

I still didn't move. Then, he said, "Move out of my way. You can use it now."

After I used the bathroom, he called me into the front room with him. Mama was still passed out in the hallway. He said, "Come here and sit on Daddy's lap."

I was scared, but he said, "Come on. I'm not going to bite you."

When I went to him, his breath smelt like gin. I knew it was gin because he and Mama drank that stuff everyday. I sat on his lap. He said, "Now, tell me. What do you want for Christmas?"

It was June. Christmas was a long time away. My real daddy was dead. I didn't comment on that, but I guess you can say he was my daddy because my real daddy wasn't around. He had been my mama's boyfriend since I could remember. He was the only daddy taking care of me. I was the only child. I told him that I wanted a Betty Boop sweater.

He said, "Sweater? You don't have anything to put in a sweater."

He said, "Get up. Let me show you something."

We then walked down the hallway to where Mama was. He pulled her shirt up and said, "You need these to wear a sweater."

He grabbed Mama's titties. Mama still didn't move.

He said, "But don't worry. I can make yours grow. Hell, I grew hers. Let's go in your room and play a grown-up game. This game will be fun. All you have to do is lay down. Pull your shirt up and watch me play with my rod. When my rod ejaculates, I'm going to squirt it on your titties, and they will grow just like your mama's. First, let me tell you the rules. You don't tell no one. It's just that simple. If you do, I'll kill you. Now, pull your shirt up. Don't make me mad. Do as I say," he said with those satanic eyes.

When I pulled up my shirt, he pulled out his rod. It was big and black. I didn't want to watch him. I didn't even want titties. All I wanted was a sweater. He was jacking his rod in front of me. He didn't even care that my bedroom didn't have a door. He just continued to jack his rod. Then, he finally let loose on my chest. It was warm, and it had a very loud smell.

He said, "The next time we play a game, I'm going to make your ass grow."

I was mad. I was mad at Mama. I was mad at God. I was mad at the world. I ran to the bathroom and scrubbed myself so hard that I had welts on my chest. I was trying to get his man sauce off of me. The next morning, Mama was still asleep in the hallway. I stepped over Mama again and went

into the kitchen to eat a bowl of cereal. I was not prepared for what I was about to see. I saw my Auntie Shirley sucking Antonio's dick. She stayed with us. She didn't stop when I walked in on them. She finished. I ran back to my room. She came in after me about 15 minutes later. She said, "Look. What you saw was me doing my job. You don't understand this, but your mama and I are prostitutes. We work for Antonio."

Auntie Shirley told me more than Mama had ever told me. They worked at a hotel alright. They were whores, and Antonio was their pimp. Mama and Auntie Shirley worked on Stewart Avenue at night.

I heard the door slam. I shoved Mama's notebook under my leg. It was Tonio flying in to get some water. No wonder Mama never talked about her mother. She was a prostitute. And we had an auntie? I wondered where she was. What else wasn't Mama telling me? Mama had had it bad like me. All I was trying to figure out was who Antonio was. Was the man in Mama's journal my daddy? I had to keep reading that journal without letting Mama find out. I had so many questions racing through my head. I put the notebook back where she had left it. I had so many questions for her. She had played grown-up games, too...

Chapter Eleven
Daddy, Can I go to Church, Please?

As the years went by, I really didn't see much of Bobby at school. He was probably still fucking Shelia. I hadn't really seen her that much at school, either. I didn't know why, but I still wanted her. One Sunday morning, after Mama and Tonio had already left for church and while I was in my room singing Patti LaBelle's "On My Own," out of no where Daddy came in, saying, "Sing it, baby."

He made his way into my room with his brown paper bag. He started singing Michael McDonald's part of the song. I was so sick and tired of fucking my daddy. He came closer, dancing his way to me and turning up his favorite pop. His breath was loud as usual.

"You know what today is, don't you?" he asked, dancing like he knew how. "You done got too old to still be playing grown-up games. You're almost grown, but you're never too grown to stop fucking your daddy." The way he said things just really got to me. How much more of this shit did I have to take? I was ready to kill him. I was 15, and Daddy was 55 at the time. I'd been playing grown-up games with him for 9 years now. When would this shit end? I did the usual. I sucked his dick right before I jumped on it and rode him like The Lone Ranger. He walked out of my room, saying, "Yeah, this old man still got it."

The next day, I went to school. We had a new student in class. Her name was Lisa McKinney. We had homeroom and Mrs. Lawrence's 2nd period math class together. We sat down at the lunch table together. I asked her where she was from. She was from Georgia, and she'd transferred from Benjamin E. Mays High. I could tell she was mixed. She looked like a life size Barbie doll. I knew she was spoiled off the bat because she had on Polo everything, even down to the book bag. I wanted us to be good friends, possibly even more. We could do each other like them ladies did each other in Daddy's porn. I wondered what it would be like to be with a girl. The porn stars made it look real good on TV. Although Lisa and I became good friends, I still thought about Shelia from time to time. I wanted Lisa to explode in my mouth like Daddy had. Later that week, I asked Mama if I could spend the night at Lisa's.

She said, "Go ask your daddy. You ask him for everything else."

Why did Mama always say that when I asked her for something? If she didn't want me, she should have just aborted me. I knew all the answers to my questions were in her notebook. I just had to get my hands on it and read as much of it as I could. When Daddy got home, I asked him if I could spend the night at Lisa's.

"No, you can't spend the night away from home," he said, downing his favorite pop. "Who is Lisa anyway? Go ask your mama and see what she says."

"I did. She told me to come and ask you," I said, licking my lips at him, "Can I, Daddy, please?"

"I'll think about it. Go in there and get my pop out the fridge."

One time, Mama came in the front room while Daddy was in there watching TV and sipping on his favorite pop. I could tell Mama hated Daddy's guts. She

53

asked, "Why don't you go to church anymore. We all need to go as a family including Tonae."

"I got my church right here in this bottle. I don't have to go to church. I know what to do. Nothing's happened to me this far. Tonae can go next Sunday. Bring her back home right after church. Don't take her to bingo with you and Tonio."

Sunday morning came, and I was ready to go to church. God didn't come to me, so I went to Him. Tonio looked nice in the suit Mama had bought for him. If you asked me, Mama was more of a daddy to Tonio than Daddy was. I always wished they could have switched roles. She took him to all his basketball games. She took him to the gym to practice his jump shot. She was the one who bought him that basketball goal. We got in Mama's '86 Buick Century. I sat in the back. The ride was silent. We passed by Bobby's house. I wondered if he was at home. I hadn't seen or talked to him. When we got to church, I was so glad. I could finally go in there and tell God to kill Daddy. Daddy had taken my whole childhood. All I knew was how to jack, suck, and fuck a dick. I was supposed to be on the cheerleading squad or at a karaoke bar, singing and getting discovered by a famous producer. Instead, for the last 9 years, I had been fucking and sucking my no good ass daddy almost everyday. When I got to the door, Pastor Riley was standing there, smiling and saying, "Well, look who the devil done brung in."

He was right. That devil was my daddy.

"Hey, Tonae. I haven't seen you in 100 years."

"I'm not 100," I replied.

"I know, but I haven't seen you in a long time."

I wanted Pastor Riley to shut the fuck up before I forgot all the stuff I had to tell God. Mama, Tonio, and I sat in a middle row. The church wasn't that big. It was

just like I had remembered, except they had Mary painted on one window, and Jesus was painted on the other. Jesus didn't want to be by Mary just like Daddy didn't want Mama. When the choir began to sing, I saw this girl who reminded me of Shelia. She was the lead singer. They sang "His Eye is on the Sparrow." She sounded just like I did back in junior high. While she sang, I pictured her singing to me. I felt she was looking at me the whole time. I was in the house of God, so why was I having these sexual feelings toward another girl? A church girl, at that. Was that what I wanted? Was I gay? Could I be with a girl? When they were done, Pastor Riley said, "Now, all my saints, stand where you are and just worship the Lord."

I didn't stand up because I didn't want everyone looking at me. Everyone else stood up. Mama whispered with her teeth shut, "Stand up."

Then, she reached over and thumped Tonio so he could wake up. I stood up to worship God, saying, "God, please come in my house and kill Daddy. You see everything. Why do I gotta keep fucking him? How come Mama can't fuck him? Well, since you can't kill Daddy, can you send the devil in to do it for you? Please, God, I'll leave the door unlocked, so he can come in."

I knew about the devil because Pastor Riley used to say, "Look at all this killing going on. It ain't nobody but the devil."

"God, please hear me. I'm tired of doing all those nasty things with Daddy and Uncle Buck. Oh yeah, God, while you're at it, can you kill Uncle Buck and Bobby Knight, too?"

Service was over, and I was feeling good. The Good Book said, "If ye ask, then ye shall receive."

Daddy had made it clear for Mama to drop me off after church. He didn't want me to go to bingo with her

and Tonio. When Mama dropped me off, I opened up the screen door and saw Daddy lying on his back. I said, "Damn, God, you work quick."

Daddy was passed out on the floor, flat on his face. My second thought was Daddy was probably just drunk as usual. But then again, maybe the devil came in and took Daddy out. I tried to shake him and wake him up, but Daddy didn't move.

"Get up, Daddy. Get up," I said.

Still nothing. Daddy was dead. I called 911. When they arrived, they pricked his finger and discovered that his blood sugar was low, and his blood pressure was high. They revived his ass with a piece of fucking peppermint. I couldn't believe that shit. All that Jack Daniels Daddy had drunk, and one small piece of peppermint brought his ass back to life.

"Mr. Watson. Mr. Watson. Can you hear me?" the paramedic asked.

"Ma'am, is your daddy a diabetic?"

"A what? No, sir."

I didn't know what the hell "a diabetic" meant. Daddy's blood pressure was 198/125. They asked if he ate a lot of sweets or drank a lot of pop.

I said, "Yes. He drinks pop everyday."

"Yeah. That'll do it," said the paramedic.

He just didn't know that the pop Daddy drank everyday was Jack Daniels, not soda pop. They took Daddy to the hospital. I wanted to go over to Lisa's house. Instead, I looked for Mama's notebook.

Chapter Twelve
Mama's Notebook

It was about 3 PM when I found Mama's notebook. I had more than enough time to read the whole notebook. I was finally about to find out what was up with Mama, and why she hated her mother so much. I took off my dress and put on a short set. I looked in the spots where Mama normally hid it, but it wasn't there. I looked on top of the fridge. It wasn't there, either. I saw it under the microwave. Bingo! I turned to the page where I had left off. The man promised Mama a Betty Boop sweater. I opened it up and some of the pages were ripped out, but I continued to read it anyway.

September 10, 1970

Big Mama came and took me to church. I was glad I was finally going to church, so I could ask God to kill Mama's live-in boyfriend, Antonio. I wish I could stay with Big Mama. I didn't want to stay with Mama anymore. I was glad to go to church. I didn't have a dress to wear, but Big Mama said, "God don't discriminate. Come as you are."

And I did just that. I put on my favorite Betty Boop t-shirt that read "superstar", a pair of wrangler jeans, and my black eyed peas. Big Mama picked me up for church. I was so glad, I was about to go to church and tell God to kill Mama's boyfriend, Antonio. I had been praying for two years now that God would kill Mama and Antonio. I was going to the church

to tell God in person. I hopped in her '68 Cadillac. She is only 55 years old. I don't know why we call her Big Mama.

When we arrived at the church, I couldn't wait for the part when the pastor said, "Now, all my saints, stand where you are and just worship the Lord."

That part of the sermon came faster than I expected. I stood up silently and said, "God, please come in my house and kill Mama's boyfriend, Antonio. Please kill Mama, too. God, if you're too busy to do it, can you send the devil to our house to do it? I really hate Auntie Shirley because the sweater Antonio was supposed to give me, he gave to her. So while you're at it, kill her ass, too. God, I hate them all. Please come in and kill them all. God, I am in your house now. The preacher said, 'If I ask, then I shall receive.' God, I know you are busy with the whole world. Just send the devil to kill them. I'll leave the door unlocked."

Service was over, and I had just spilled my insides to God. I know He heard me this time. Big Mama dropped me back off with Mama and Antonio. She didn't even come in. She didn't approve of Mama's lifestyle from what I heard Mama telling Antonio. She was the same way until she gave her life to God. Big Mama knew what was going on. She hated that Antonio was fucking all three of us — Mama, Auntie Shirley, and me.

I had tears in my eyes. I couldn't believe Mama had gone through the same shit I was going through. Mama didn't even have a dress to wear to church. Mama and I had said some similar prayers to God. I didn't know I had an auntie. Mama never talked about her. Where was she? And where was Big Mama, who would be my great-grandma? Damn it! Was history repeating itself? Mama had gotten fucked by her step-daddy, and I was getting fucked by my real daddy. No wonder Mama was cool with Daddy fucking me. What the hell was wrong with her and her mama? Now, I had to find out if

the Antonio in Mama's journal was my daddy because he was much older than Mama. The door slammed shut, and I put the notebook back up. I walked into the front room. From the way Mama was looking, I knew she had got the news about Daddy. I couldn't figure out why the fuck she was crying. He should have died. If I had known they were going to save his ass with a piece of peppermint, I would not have dialed 911 right away. Mama said that she heard from Mrs. Lawrence that Daddy was in the hospital. Ever since Mrs. Lawrence had seen me in that Patti dress, she'd been trying to get at Daddy. How the fuck did mama feel knowing that Daddy was so disoriented that he gave them Mrs. Lawrence phone number instead of Uncle Buck's? If Daddy was fucking me and she did nothing, she really didn't care if he fucked my teacher, too.

Mama asked us to go with her. I didn't want to go, and Tonio didn't want to go either. Tonio and I looked at each other, and we told her that we didn't want to go. I could have went with Daddy when the ambulance came, but I chose to stay and read Mama's notebook. Mama said, "Fine. Then, don't go."

Tonio wasn't too fond of Daddy because he hadn't done shit for him. She knew I didn't care because he'd been fucking my brains out since I was ten years old. Tonio and I fell asleep on the living room sofa.

Chapter Thirteen
Daddy's Home to Stay

Daddy was in the hospital for three weeks. I felt like a virgin. It felt good not to have Daddy digging in my pussy. If I didn't fuck him when he wanted or if I acted like I didn't want it, he'd say, "You know I'm the only one who loves you. I buy you everything you ask for. Your mama don't care about you."

Daddy was right because, if she loved me, she wouldn't have let Daddy keep fucking me. I was glad he wasn't at home to suck on my nipples like a lollipop.

Mama came flying in the house, saying, "Y'all come and help me get Daddy."

My first thought was, *Why couldn't he have just died in the hospital? That is the place where people sometimes just die. But not my daddy. He refused to die.*

For those last three weeks, Tonio and I were all good. Then, everything changed when Daddy came home.

Mama said that I would have to take care of Daddy because he was too weak to take care of himself. I had been taking care of Daddy all these years, so why stop now? Tonio and I helped him into the house. He had lost weight, and his salt and pepper colored hair had matted up all over his head. I couldn't believe Daddy was so weak. He looked as if he had shrunk. We laid

him on the sofa in the front room. Mama told me that I would have to give Daddy insulin shots in his stomach. Daddy was diagnosed with diabetes and high blood pressure. I asked, "What is insulin?"

Mama explained that Daddy didn't have enough in his body, and I had to inject it into him with a needle. I told Mama, "Sure, I'd love to take care of Daddy."

While Daddy slept on the sofa, Tonio and Mama went to the store. I went to go read Mama's notebook.

August 4, 1971

Shit hasn't changed. Antonio and Mama are still alive. I hate them so much. So far the devil and God haven't answered my prayers. Mama has really gotten loose over the years. She loves Antonio so much that she wants to have a baby with him, but that is impossible because Mama is sterile from a pelvic inflammatory disease. But what if she could have kids? If it was a boy, would Antonio fuck him, too? I hate him. I hate Mama. I hate God. I hate the devil. I hate myself. Mama has got to be crazy to have a baby with him. My pussy is raw right now because he sticks all types of shit in me like I'm plastic not flesh. Sometimes when I haven't fully healed from the rawness, he'll come in my room, look at my pussy, and say, "You'll be ready in a few more days, just suck my dick for now."

I hate him so bad that I wish I had razors for teeth. He is my Mad from Inspector Gadget, except there is no "Until next time, Gadget." He always finds something for me to do. I remember the first time he introduced me to that shit that he put in Mama's arm. He didn't put it in my arm. He made me taste it and sniff it. It made my nose burn and throw up.

When I threw up, Antonio said, "Yes, that's it — Grade A."

This man is the devil in the flesh, getting my fourteen year old ass hooked on heroin. Now, when I say hooked, I didn't have to work on Stewart Avenue like Mama and Auntie

Shirley. Antonio practically feeds it to me. One Saturday night, we were in the basement. All of us were stoned. There was blue lights flashing, and Mama was really stoned. Antonio went to get some gin and Mama came to me and gave me a hot shot. This is when you get the drugs intravenously. Antonio would give them to me. I was hooked on snorting them; but Mama was so stoned that she put the needle in my arm anyway. When Antonio got back, I was nodding in and out. I was so high. All I remember is Antonio coming in there, and Mama giving me more gin. Mama asked me if I would have their child. I started to sweat. I was mad at both of them. I was mad at Antonio for getting me hooked, and I was mad at Mama for giving me to her man. By the time the drugs kicked in, I was down for whatever. Antonio wasn't my real daddy; but, high on the drugs, I'd say, "Daddy, give me some more. Give me more. Yes, Daddy, yes. I'll have your baby."

I couldn't read any more of this shit. Was Antonio Mama's step-daddy, too? Antonio was my daddy. I bet this was the same man that Mama was talking about in her journal. The more I read, the more I didn't want to know. I skipped some pages and went to Mama's poetry.

Poem Number One:

One Free Night

Lying in my room all alone,
Mama and her boyfriend wasn't at home.
Although I'm scared in this house with no one here,
I wish they wouldn't come back none this year.
Mama was dead wrong for the shit she did
My body from her boyfriend she didn't try to get rid
Antonio isn't here to touch me tonight

I wish I had Big Mama's number so I could get out of
sight.

Antonio has been touching me since I was six.
God, do you think my broken heart you can fix?
I'm crying out to you, and it hurts so much.
Damn, I wish my real daddy would have stayed in
touch.

Poem Number Two:

Xmas Night

Christmas night was fun and games
But I didn't have one present under the tree with my
name.

Antonio said I've been a bad girl the whole year.
I wasn't listening to him, covering up my ears.
I wonder if Mama even knew my real dad.
Growing up all these years, I've been so sad.
I wonder if Mama loves me, and, if she do,
How come she didn't do the things her boyfriend made
me do?

Being around that man really creeps me out.
When I get older, I'll be able to shout! Shout! Shout!
But that wouldn't do any good and this I know
Mama gave me to her boyfriend years ago.

Poem Number Three:

Auntie Shirley

Auntie Shirley was no better than Mom
She loved to watch Mama's boyfriend cum
All over her neck and sometimes her face
Auntie Shirley is always in Antonio's lap
Deep down inside her face I wanted to slap

To make her realize that all this shit Antonio is doing
to us isn't right
But then all that would do is start a fight
Satan, I prayed to God that Antonio would stay from
under my skirt
But, Satan, God is too busy. Can you please come and
do your dirty work?

Poem Number Four:

I Hate the Most

God, of all the things I hate the most,
When Mama comes to hell make sure her soul you'll
roast.
All these years she's been living a lie.
God, please let Mama and her boyfriend die.
I know this is all wrong, and I shouldn't say,
But I'm a little girl who can't even go outside and play
Her boyfriend always had his way with me
I wish I was brave enough to kill myself
I wish I could destroy all their drugs on the top shelf
I don't understand why Mama does the things she does
I would be happy if she said, "Daughter, I love you."
My Big Mama says she loves me so much.
If she did, then why doesn't she keep in touch?
Mama's boyfriend keeps fucking me, and it's never
going to end.
Damn, I wish I had something nice to write with this
pen.

Poem Number Five:

My Nightly Prayer

Now, I lay me down to sleep
God, make sure Antonio dies in your keep
If I die before I awake
God, please let my real daddy be in heaven with my
favorite cake
All this stuff doesn't even make sense?
All Antonio's filth on my body I wish I could just rinse
When I do go to school, I can't even learn
Because Antonio is always taking my body for a turn
When I get grown, I don't ever want a boyfriend.
I can't wait until Antonio's life comes to an end.
How many times do I have to pray?
God, Big Mama, somebody, come and take me away.

Chapter Fourteen
Writing Contest

Two years had passed and I felt like a virgin because Daddy was too sick to put his nasty dick in me. I was in the 12th grade. My favorite class was Mr. Wright's writing class. One day, our assignment was to write a poem about anything. My poem was called **"Dad, Dad."**

Dad, dad,
What can I say?
You were 26 and Mom was 14 years young
        being your prey
I was told this and I was told that
But you having sex with my mama and auntie was a
known fact
You had my auntie and then my mom
Damn, Dad, how many times did you have to cum?
I know back in the days was all fun and play
Didn't you think all this shit would come out one day
I know the truth; and yes, it hurts.
But, Dad, I forgive you. I want to make it work.
Growing up, fucking you was bad enough
So I did drugs, had sex to cover the pain up.
The End

Mr. Wright didn't take points off for my grammar because he was so impressed with the poem itself.

"Tonae, your poem seems so real," he said.

"I know."

Little did he know that it was all the truth.

"That's good work. How did you do that? How long did it take for you to write this?"

"Five minutes."

"Five minutes?"

"Yes."

"Well, quick. Make something up now with my name."

"Mr. Wright, Mr. Wright,
The next man touch me
I'll take his life."

"Wow. That's deep." He smiled at me.

"So, do I get an A?"

"No, you get an E," he said. "My mother's in the hospital. Do you think you can hook her up a line or two?"

"Sure, Mr. Wright. I'd be glad to."

"How long will it take?"

"I'll be done by the end of the day."

"What's wrong with your mother?"

"The doctors say she has cancer."

"Oh, Mr. Wright, I'm sorry to hear that. I'll have it for you at three o'clock."

During senior year, a lot of us had changed. Lisa McKinney didn't wear Polo anymore. She was more casual. She really looked sophisticated. I wanted her even more. Daddy never did let me spend the night over at her house in the tenth grade. So since he was sick, and Mama didn't care, I could go whenever I was ready. She really looked like a porn star. I asked Lisa at lunch if she wanted some company after school. At first, she looked puzzled.

"Sure. Why not?"

I said, "What you can't have black people at your house?"

"Don't be silly. It's just you wanted to come so many times before and never did."

"Well, a lot has changed since then."

She looked so good. I wanted to throw her on the lunch table and eat her pussy like I was eating the inside of an orange, sucking and swallowing everything.

"What do you want to do over at my house?"

"We can sing," I lied. I knew how to sing like Patti. I just wanted to get close to her. I couldn't have Shelia, and I hadn't even seen her in a long time. I hadn't seen Bobby. Maybe they had moved in together and had kids, maybe even got married. Who knew? At the end of the day, I gave Mr. Wright his poem for his mom. It read:

Dear Mama,
You're just taking a little rest
God wanted you to chill out because He knows best
You need to just lie down and rest your bones
When you get better, I'll be at your home
To take care of you like you took care of me
Now that's how a mother and son are supposed to be
You're my pride and joy, and you can not go
Mama, God has always loved us both
I hate the bad news the doctors had to say
So every night I get down on my knees and continue to
pray
The doctors say it's cancer and that you're dying
I don't believe them doctors one bit; they're all just
lying.
You gotta fight this battle for yourself
God have mercy on you and give you back your health
I'm crushed inside and feel like my heart is still
You leaving this earth is not a part of God's will.

Mr. Wright's eyes watered, and he started to cry. "I can't believe I'm crying in front of one of my students."

"It's okay, Mr. Wright."

His eyes said thanks a lot. "This is a deep poem, and it fits us. You really should enter the poetry contest at the Fox Theater."

"No, thanks. I'm going to be a singer. Watch out, Patti," I said.

We both laughed. I headed to Lisa's house. I didn't have to worry about giving Daddy his insulin 'cause Mama was there.

Chapter Fifteen
Lisa McKinney's House

When I got to Lisa's house, she was at the door. She had on a white halter top and a short skirt. She had a nice tan, too. Every time I saw her, I thought about the porn I watched with Daddy. She had a big pretty house. It looked small from the outside, but once I got in there, it was huge. It had 16 ft cathedral ceilings with marble floors. I thought Daddy had spoiled me. This girl was super spoiled. She almost had more clothes than Tonio and me put together. When we got in her room, she had a big picture on the wall of her daddy. She stressed that she loved him dearly. I wondered if she had to fuck him for all this shit. I wondered if I was the only girl fucking her daddy. She told me that her daddy had died and left her mama a nice insurance policy. She also said her mama gave her $2,000.00 a month. That explained the Mercedes she drove to school. Her mother worked for IBM. After I'd been there a few minutes, Lisa's mom came in her room.

"Oh, I didn't know you had company."

"Yes. Now you see. What is it? And next time, knock."

I never understood why some white kids talked back to their parents. If that would have been me, Daddy would have beat my ass and then fucked me. Some kids would kill to have a mother like Lisa's, and one of those

kids was me. Mama hardly said two fucking words to me.

"Okay, Mom. This is Tonae. Tonae, meet my mom."

I smiled and said, "Nice to meet you, Ms. McKinney."

"Mom, she's going to spend the night."

Just like that. She didn't ask her. She told her. If that was me telling Daddy something, he would have slapped me and made me suck his dick afterwards.

"You, girls, have fun. I'm going out. Call me on my cell if you need me," she said as she left.

Lisa said, "Yeah, like that'll ever happen."

Why am I still thinking about Daddy's sick ass? I'm trying to make this girl my special friend, maybe my girlfriend, if that's possible. We both were serious about graduating. Lisa was an A-student, too.

Despite my dysfunctional family, I kept my grades up because, once I was out of school, I planned on going to college AS FAR AWAY FROM DADDY AS I COULD. We were damn near grown. Whatever we did, I hoped Lisa could keep quiet about it.

"So, Miss Tonae, what is it that you wanna do?"

I could get used to my fans saying my name like that once I was famous.

"Do you wanna sing?" I said, knowing deep down inside I wanted to sex her.

"Yeah, let's sing on my karaoke machine."

I was singing my heart out. Finally, she said, "Girl, I can't sing."

She playfully hit me with a pillow dead in my face.

I said, "Oh, it's on now." I grabbed two pillows and got her back. Then, I started tickling her. Her titties were bouncing up and down in that halter top. I got

moist between my legs. My pussy was soaking wet. All I could think about was the women in Daddy's porn. I was tickling her until she was pink in the face. Then, she said, "Surrender. I give up."

As soon as I stopped, she attacked me and started tickling me. She got on top of me, and I laughed until I almost wet my pants. It felt good feeling her soft hands all on me. I loved the warmth of her hands all over my stomach and rib cage. She looked so pretty with that Colgate smile. I finally stopped laughing and asked if she wanted to play a game.

"Sure," she said, lying down beside me on her bed and looking up at the ceiling. "What kind of game?"

I said, "You'll like this game," while taking off my shirt and leaving on nothing but my Adidas sports bra and shorts. "It's a grown up game called 'touch and feel.'"

"'Touch and feel'? How do you play a game called 'touch and feel?'"

I sounded like Daddy and Uncle Buck.

"Well, we can start the game off by sipping some of this." I pulled out a brown paper bag with Daddy's favorite pop in it. Jack had been my daddy's best friend for years. Eventually, I had picked up the same habit.

"What's this?" she asked, grabbing the bottle out of my hand. "Do your parents know you drink?"

"My daddy does; my mama doesn't care what I do."

"Why do you say your mama doesn't care?" She turned the bottle up to her lips.

"She just doesn't. Okay? I need to be asking you. Does your mama know you drink? You just turned that bottle up like you're no amateur."

"I'm not. I been drinking since my daddy died. My mama knows. All she did was send me to counseling, which didn't help at all."

I didn't want to go into detail about her dad's death because all I had on my mind was that porn I used to watch with my daddy.

I said, "Here are the rules. You can't tell anyone." I was really sounding like Daddy.

"Girl, I'm not going to tell nobody," she said, taking her shirt off. "I'm hot. Are you hot?" she asked.

She was getting used to Jack because she turned the bottle up and said, "Let the games begin."

I said, "Okay, you go first."

She was eyeing my stomach.

"That's easy," I said, "You're looking at my stomach."

She said, "Nope. You're wrong. I'm looking at your navel."

She came over and stuck her tongue in my navel. My pussy got wet in an instant.

"Okay, Miss Tonae. It's your turn."

I stared at her face. She turned up the bottle and said, "Yours is easy, too. You're looking at my face."

I said, "Nope. You're wrong. I'm looking at your lips."

I walked over and kissed her on the mouth. She was kind of shocked but not totally.

"I never done it with a girl before."

"Hell, I haven't done it with a boy," she said, smiling and twirling her hair.

I didn't tell her I had fucked Bobby, so I just let her think I was a virgin, too. It was her turn. She looked at the side of my head. I said, "You are looking at my head."

She said, "Nope, I'm looking at your ears." She licked my ears in a circular motion, and my clit jumped. I was feeling horny, and Jack had kicked in. The game turned me on. I looked at her chest, and she said, "Okay. Now, I see you are looking at my titties."

I said, "Yep. Can I suck them?"

She said, "Hell, yeah. Our secret, remember?"

Her nipples were pink just like them women in the porn I watched with Daddy. I licked them both at the same time. She was rolling and moving like a fish. I whispered, "Does it feel good?"

She said, "Hell, yeah."

I said, "Do you want me to stop?"

She said, "Hell, no."

I kept licking her titties. She grabbed my hand and put it under her skirt. She said, "It's my turn."

By this time, my pussy was throbbing. She stopped and looked at my hand. I said, "You are looking at my hand."

"Nope." She grabbed my hand and licked my middle finger, put it in her pussy, and then in my mouth. I got to admit that she tasted pure, not salty like Daddy and Bobby. We took off our clothes. I was drunk, and she was too.

"Are you sure you haven't done this before?" Lisa asked.

"I'm sure, but I have seen it on TV."

She said she had, too.

I had wanted Shelia to be my first girl, but my dream was finally about to come true—to see what it was like to be with a girl. When we got in her bed, I was the aggressor. I wanted her more. I really didn't care if she did me or not. I had just wanted to do this for a long time now. First, we just kissed. Then, I made my way down to her titties. Then, I went down to the sea to lick

her pearl. I sucked her clit like it was a chicken leg with no meat. I opened up and found the little man in the boat. Lisa screamed my name and moaned. I kept licking her clit. First, fast. Then, slow. Then, down and side to side until all her juices went into my mouth. I swallowed everything. Daddy had taught me good. I didn't spill anything.

She said, "Damn, I never had that feeling before. What were you doing down there?"

I asked her to be my girlfriend, and she said, "How could I be with anyone else after experiencing what I just felt?"

We drifted off to sleep. I thought for once I had someone who wouldn't take advantage of me, and it felt good.

Chapter Sixteen
Taking Care of Daddy

I really didn't want to shoot Daddy with insulin. I wanted to shoot him with a gun. Daddy always had this funny look on his face when I lifted up his shirt to give him his shot in his stomach. Daddy was a serious diabetic. He had to have the sugar injected properly in his stomach. I remember one day, as I was giving him his shot, his eyes were blood shot red. As soon as he got a little strength, he was back to his old ways. He didn't care what the doctors said. He kept drinking his favorite pop.

"Daddy, you have to stop drinking," I said, acting like I gave a fuck.

"I'll worry about Jack, and you worry about that sugar shot."

I didn't want Daddy to just up and die. I wanted to have the pleasure of getting revenge on him. I wanted to watch him scream, just like I did when he first took my innocence. I screamed and not even God heard my cries. I wanted to see Daddy suffer. He sat up in the bed, and I gave him his shot. He joked and said, "You know my dick don't get hard anymore. I asked your mama to suck it, and it just went limp. Let's see if you can get it hard."

I couldn't believe this man. He still wanted me to fuck him. I reached in his pants and pulled it out. He

had gray hair down there. I tried to get his dick hard, but it didn't grow.

He said, "I thought it was your mama, but it's you, too. What the hell? Since you're down there, you might as well suck it."

I had been hearing 'suck it' for 9 years. Even though Daddy's dick wasn't hard, I sucked it like a pro. He finally came, but I didn't swallow it. I spit it on his stomach.

"It's been a long time. You still know how to make your daddy happy," he said, wiping his man sauce off his stomach.

I had no choice. I had to take care of Daddy until I came up with a plot to kill him. He had no idea of the type of pain he was causing me. I wondered what Uncle Buck was doing. I wondered if the devil or God had killed him yet. He hadn't been around to see Daddy since he'd been sick. Mama didn't comb Daddy's hair. It was still matted up. He didn't want Mama to do anything for him. He didn't even want her to sleep with him. He made her sleep in the front room on the sofa. I knew I had to finish reading Mama's notebook. I had to find out if the "Antonio" in her journal was my daddy. I needed to know if my daddy was Mama's step-daddy.

Chapter Seventeen
Mama's Notebook—Blue Lights Flashing

I continued to read Mama's notebook where I had left off. Mama's mama had asked her to carry a child for her and her boyfriend.

September 5, 1971

> *The night I was with Mama and her boyfriend in the basement, I was very high. Mama gave me hot shots in the arm, and Antonio gave me bumps of heroin in my nose. He kept saying, "Here, chase it with this gin."*
>
> *Mama was so stoned. She kept saying, "My baby can handle this."*
>
> *We were lying on a bed in the basement, listening to Al Green's "Love and Happiness". Whenever I hear that song, it reminds me of the threesome we all had together — Mama, her boyfriend, and me. Mama kept saying, " I can't wait until you have this baby for us."*
>
> *I was so stoned. Blue lights were flashing everywhere. I felt like I was floating on clouds in outer space. Mama asked if I wanted to get high. I wondered how high I could get. She kept giving me shots of heroin and gin all night long. We all laid in the bed. Mama rubbed her hands through my hair, saying, "Baby, this isn't going to hurt. You know I love you, right?"*
>
> *If this was love, I don't want it anymore. What could hurt me? Because Antonio and I had slept together plenty*

times before. Mama pulled my pants down and said, "You're going to give us a beautiful baby."

I was so high. I was nodding my head. I wanted to say something, but my mouth couldn't speak words. I wanted to cry, but tears couldn't even flow down my face. I was so numb. I just laid there. Then, Antonio came and pulled my shirt up, licking my nipples and saying, "I told you I could make them grow."

I was only eleven. I still had nubs from when he played the first grown-up game with me. I wanted to scream but again no words could come out. All I could do was just lay there and let them have their way with me. Mama was so stoned. She didn't realize that she was sliding her fingers in and out my pussy, playing with it. She said, "Nay, Nay, when you have this baby for us, it'll be just like yours; but, since you're so young, we'll have to take care of it."

Mama was so in love with this man that she gave her only daughter to him to satisfy his needs. I was out of it. The room was spinning. Antonio told Mama to come up to the top and suck my titties. Mama turned up that bottle of gin and did what Antonio told her to do. I wanted to get up and run, but I was too stoned to do anything. While Antonio was fucking me, Mama was sitting on my face saying, "Eat this pussy. Eat it."

I didn't know nothing about eating no pussy, and I had to eat my mama's pussy. How crazy was that? When it was all over, I had vague memories of the night before. When I woke up, I was sick from all the bullshit my body had consumed. Mama was gone on her hoe stroll. Antonio was there looking at me. I felt a different vibe from him, and I was right. He told me that once I had the child, he was going to make me his wife. I said, "What about Mama?"

He said, "Don't worry about her. She's washed up, and I want you."

I asked him if he was going to put me on Stewart Avenue. He told me that he wanted me to have this child and get back into school. His whole demeanor had changed. He

wanted us to be a family without Mama. When he left that morning, I got up, went to the bathroom, looked in the mirror, and made up a poem called "Pain."

Pain

Pain, oh, God, it hurts so bad.
You see, my life, it's so sad.
I'm a little girl and can't have fun
I wish I had the courage to leave home and run
I write a lot of poems when I'm drunk and high,

But all this shit is true. I keep it real. Why lie?
I write and write and keep it real.
Hoping to God that one day all this pain He'll heal.
I'm carrying a child now, and it's not easy
Looking back on history all my ancestors was sleazy.
Yeah, you frown and say, "How can I say that?"
Not even my mama had my back.
One day all this hurt and pain will be heard
And no, I'm not just another person that's disturbed...

After crying my heart out to God, I thought, Why should I give my baby to them? Mama don't love me. And Antonio don't even love Mama. All he cares about is the money that she and Auntie Shirley bring him from prostituting on Stewart Avenue. That's why Mama couldn't have no more kids because she was sleeping with all them different men. She had gotten a bad infection. When she finally did go to the doctor, it was too late. Her fallopian tubes were badly bruised. She was sterile from then on.

I don't want to have this baby, but it's too late. And if it's a girl, I want to comb her hair just like I used to do my baby doll. I want to be able to protect her from Mama and Antonio. If I run away, where will I go? I want to keep my

80

baby from them. They might have a threesome with her. Antonio might make her start sucking his dick when she turns ten like he did me.

One night, while I was 8 ½ months pregnant, Antonio came in my room. He was going on about how he was tired of Mama. She was out there just fucking men and not bringing him any money. She was doing it just for the high. He said, "You're still young and tender. Maybe after you have our baby, you can go work on Stewart Avenue, too."

He said that he'd gotten us an apartment on Cleveland Avenue, not too far from Stewart Avenue. Mama was 26 and Antonio was too, but I was 14 and carrying their child.

When I want into labor, Mama was out in the streets. Antonio was at home with me. We had just got through having sex. He fucked me so hard from the back. When he finished, I went to the bathroom and all this yucky stuff started flowing down my legs.

He said, "Let's go. It's time."

We went to Grady Hospital. I wanted Antonio to give me a fix in my arm so bad so all this pain could go away. We went in, and the nurses asked him if was he my father and where my mother was. He said, "I'm her step-dad."

They checked me, saying, "Yeah, she's ready to deliver. She's already 9 centimeters."

Antonio was right there holding my hand. He wasn't so bad. He kept saying, "Just breath slowly." They put tubes in my nose and gave me an IV. The tubes were for oxygen and the IV was to keep fluid in my body so that I would stay hydrated. The doctor was in front and Antonio and the nurse had one of my legs each pushing them toward my chest. I pushed and screamed. It felt like my pussy was on fire. At first, I thought I had shitted myself. Then, I heard a loud cry.

"It's a girl!"

Antonio said that he would marry me and take care of me and our child.

"What about Mama?"

"She's dead."

"Dead?"

"Yes. To you. Let her be dead."

When I gave birth to our child, Antonio changed. He didn't have any other kids.

He said, "Let's name her Tonae Ann Watson."

I stopped reading Mama's journal. My daddy, Antonio, was also her step-daddy. That explains why he is so much older than her. She ran away with him when she had me.

Chapter Eighteen
Antonio Stopped Pimping

June 3, 1972

When I got out of the hospital, Antonio had an apartment ready. It was better than Mama's house. Our baby was so pretty. Antonio had decided that he didn't want me to work on Stewart Avenue after all. He had gotten a job at General Motors while I stayed at home trying to take care of our baby. The nurse knew I was pretty young. She gave me pamphlets and videos on how to hold and feed and change a baby. Antonio was at home everyday with a brown paper bag around 6 PM. He didn't drink gin anymore nor did he do anymore drugs. I asked him to get me some but that only pissed him off, so I was drug-free, too. He would go straight to Tonae's crib and wake her up. She was a good baby. I used to hold her all day in my arms until he got home. He'd either take her from me or wake her in her crib. Even though Antonio was working and taking care of us, he'd gotten mean all of a sudden. All he wanted when he got home from work was Tonae. Once while we were at Target getting her some clothes, a lady was in front of the store passing out flyers and asking that we come to her church. I have been going to church ever since. One day while Antonio was at work and Tonae was asleep in her crib, I got a notebook and started writing poems to God and often kept a journal, too. One poem was directed straight to Mama:

When I grow up, do I gotta be just like you?
Just quickly end my life so I'll be through.
You had a mother and still did me wrong.
Damn why couldn't you just pretend to be strong.
Just kill me in the noon time
So I can arrive in heaven with a smile
They say life's a bitch and then you die.
Mom, you shouldn't have spent so much of your time getting high
Don't bring me in this world if you're not sure
That your heart will love me unconditionally and pure.
It's the same shit just a different day
Mom, why did you have to act like a female dog gone astray?

What if Mama's mama had killed her? Then I wouldn't have been here. Nor would I have had to suck my Mom's step-daddy's dick. And I wouldn't have had to suck Uncle Buck's short, fat, two-tone dick, either. I wouldn't have had to suck Bobby's dick, either. Well, I would probably have sucked Bobby's because we were the same age. All the while, I was sucking and fucking Daddy. She knew it was going on. Now, I wondered if I should kill Mama, too?

Chapter Nineteen
Mr. Wright's Story Contest

I had gotten tired of reading Mama's fucked up journal. I went to school feeling bad. I was so shocked. I couldn't believe Mama let this go on and was still letting Daddy fuck me. Mr. Wright was so impressed with my past writing assignments that he had told the whole class to write a story about whatever or however we felt. It could be real or fantasy, as long as we expressed ourselves. Reading Mama's journal, I saw where I got my talent from. She was a good writer, too. It took me less than five minutes to write my story. I stood up in front of the class. Because we were seniors, Mr. Wright knew that the grammar would be a little explicit. I tried not to use too much French. My story read:

Hi! My name is Tonae Ann Watson.
I want to kill my daddy. He has done so much to my mother and me these past years. I wish he would get sick and be left in my care. I wish he would become a diabetic with high blood pressure and low blood sugar. I want his sugar to be so low that I have to inject insulin shots. I want my mama to die, too. One Sunday morning, I had gotten tired of Daddy's shit. Finally, my wish had come true. Daddy had a stroke. I had to inject him with insulin. Well, at least, that's what he thought I'd given him. I put household bleach in Daddy's syringe and injected a little in his arm. He was just lying there like a hit

puppy, helpless. I enjoyed toying around with the calculator and the remote to the TV. I picked up the remote and pressed 911.

"Oops. That's not a phone."

Daddy had begun to foam at the mouth. So, I gave him another hit of bleach, just how he did Mama when she was only eleven years old. It felt good to take advantage of Daddy, just how he had done me all those years.

Daddy was sweating and squirming like an earthworm. He wasn't dead. He could hear me. He was talking with his eyes looking at the syringe.

"Aww, poor daddy. Do you need your insulin? Do you feel like you're going to die? Do you want me to suck your dick now? You think, if I suck it, it'll save your life? Or better yet, do you want me to put in a nasty tape and do what they're doing on TV to you?"

I gotta admit. It felt good watching Daddy lay there like he had seen God Himself.

"Daddy, can you hear me? How does that bleach feel? Does it feel good to die slow? You want me to ride your dick, huh?"

I unzipped Daddy's pants. His dick was limp and to the side.

"I remember you liked both. Yeah, I'll suck it first. Then, I'll ride you 'til you die. Yeah, that's not a bad idea. Yeah, I think that's what I'll do."
Daddy was shaking and trembling.

"What's wrong? The game isn't over yet. You're not scared, are you?"

I was sucking his dick. He tried to grab me, but he was too weak. After that, I took my pants off and put his soft dick in my soaking wet pussy.

"Damn, Daddy, your dick is too soft to ride. I need it harder."

I reached under his bed, looking for his pump. He had ordered it as a tool he used to get his dick hard. I also got his

brown paper bag and turned up the bottle of Jack. I put the syringe on the dresser and began to pump his dick up.

"There. That's a nice boy. Sound familiar, Daddy? Do you remember all those times you told me I was a good girl for getting your dick hard. Well, thank me now, Daddy."

I got the syringe off the dresser and jumped on Daddy's dick. I was on top of him riding him hard. Finally, he came; and so did his last breath. Daddy died while I was on top of him.

The End

Mr. Wright was so disturbed with my story. He called to have a meeting with Mama and Daddy.

Chapter Twenty
Parent-Teacher Meeting

I had read enough to know that my daddy, Antonio, was Mama's step-daddy. However, I wanted to know more info. When I did kill Daddy, I knew it would all have been worth it. I noticed a couple more of her pages were torn out, so I read a poem that I had decided to use in my next writing contest. Her poem was called "Only a Child."

Mama was in the kitchen. I told her that Mr. Wright wanted to have a conference with her and Daddy. She went on and on about how she didn't have time and how Daddy couldn't come at all because he was bedridden. I was glad because I didn't want the shit to hit the fan, yet. I wanted Mr. Wright to just mind his business and find my work as only a fantasy. He didn't go for it one bit. He saw how I'd always been distant in conversations about family. I really used to talk about my brother, Tonio, a lot. Tonio and I were complete opposites, but I loved him more than Mama and Daddy. Mama asked me what Mr. Wright wanted to see them about. I told her that he was preparing me for college and wanted to know their insights and ideas. I lied because I didn't want Mama to go up there. She never went all these years, so it didn't make a difference for her to start going now. Daddy was the only parent that went to the school. Mama didn't want to fake the funk. How

could she let Daddy do this to me? Did she know about Uncle Buck, too? I had to read more of her notebook. I had to put it back so she would keep writing. I couldn't let her know that I knew all of this right now. I wondered if she had slept with Uncle Buck, too. I wondered if she and Antonio really did go to church and bingo. I really wanted to kill all three of them—Mama, Daddy, and Uncle Buck. I didn't know why Daddy was the way he was. He had come from a good family. That was what Mama said. Daddy was born and raised on the Westside. He grew up in Dixie Hills. Mama told me that he always had good jobs, but that was a lie. According to her journal, he had pimped her mama and auntie. Daddy's parents were dead. His siblings were around, but they didn't keep in touch. He always used to say, "If my brothers walked through that door right now, I wouldn't know who they were. But if they whipped out their dicks, I'd know them because that's what the Watson boys are known for—big dicks!"

I hated him so much, but I couldn't complain because he gave me everything a girl could want.

I was wearing Guess and Polo and Izod. I didn't have to wear K-mart clothes and white girl tennis shoes. So, instead of looking like a bum child, I continued to do as told by Daddy and accept him for the man he was and continue to pray that God would end all this shit one day.

Only a Child

How do you think it makes me feel
When you're touching me and rubbing
Me in places that shouldn't be
Revealed? How and why did it have
To be me? When in fact behind bars &
In prison is where you should be.
Writing poetry helps me learn my
Respect and dignity you'll never earn.
You were older, and yes you know I
Was too young to be touched from the get-go.
Oh, when, oh when will this shit end?
With my life story, I don't know where to begin
I'm an adult now, and, yes, it's hard.
Those men shouldn't have come near me
From the start
I'm all grown with kids of my own
I just hope I can protect them 'til
They're grown.
When you look in the mirror and
Smile, just remember that I was only
A fucking child!!!!!

Chapter Twenty-One
Daddy's Health Improving

It seemed to me that Daddy was getting better. Mama had me to take care of my daddy. He had been her man all these years, and I would finally have the pleasure to kill him myself. Mama and Tonio were gone. It was just Daddy and me at home. He was in his room watching TV and drinking his favorite pop.

"Tonae, come here."

"Yes," I said, knowing all along he wanted to fuck.

It had been a while since we had done anything, but this was my chance to get rid of him once and for all.

"Come here and give me a quickie before your mama gets back."

"Aren't you tired of having sex with me?"

"Are you tired of my money?"

"You're just doing what a daddy is supposed to do."

"You're just like your mama. Always gotta have the last word and be sassy."

I was 17 years old, and enough was enough. I hadn't given Daddy his insulin shot, yet.

I said, "Speaking of Mama, why didn't you just stay with my grandmother and leave Mama alone? Why did y'all have to have me? Where is my grandma anyway? Do I look like her?"

"Yes. You do look exactly like her, but she had gone so far off on those drugs, and she drank so much gin that she died of liver cancer about 5 years ago."

I couldn't even cry because, in Mama's journal, she was no better than Daddy. He told me that he was a pimp and Mama's mama and her sister worked for him.

I said, "I know. What makes Mama so different? Why didn't you send her on Stewart Avenue, too?"

"Once you was born, my heart changed. I wanted to raise you as my daughter, and I wanted to have sex with you because you look so much like your grandmother. I loved her so much."

"Well, I'm not her."

"Tonae, she plotted all of this, and she got hooked on those drugs."

"You was giving her those drugs, so don't blame it on her."

"So where is Big Mama and Mama's sister, Shirley?"

"I don't know. Last I heard, Big Mama was sick, and Shirley was still on Stewart Avenue. I had your mama all those years. Once you was born, I wanted you to be your Grandmother Pat. Patricia was her name."

"Does Mama know that her mama is dead?"

"Your mama has always said that she was dead long before she died."

"Well, why did you make me play grown-up games since I was six?"

"Like I said, you looked just like Pat, and I wanted you to be her."

"Damn, Daddy, I'm your daughter. Look at me. I'm so hurt from you fucking me since I was 12. Y'all thought I was pregnant by Bobby Knight. I wasn't. I was pregnant by you. Mama took me to the clinic to get a

'wash out', which I later found out was an abortion. Daddy, I was pregnant by you!"

"Don't raise your voice at me!"

He had no idea I was about to kill his ass, but how?

"I'm sorry, Daddy. I just want some answers. I'm expressing myself. None of this makes sense to me."

I have a family full of whores, dope fiends, and alcoholics. I wished I was able to raise my grandma from the dead and ask her why she let her boyfriend fuck Mama. She had definitely put a curse on our family. Daddy didn't care that I was hurt. He was ready to fuck.

"Daddy, I'll be right back."

I stopped outside Daddy's door and broke down. We had never talked. All we had ever done was fuck. Now, I knew Daddy was fucking me because I looked so much like my grandma.

I wanted to find something harmful to put in Daddy's syringe. I went in my room and grabbed my nail polish remover, but that smell was too strong. I didn't want Daddy to smell it and get suspicious. I walked by Tonio's room to see if he had anything. He only had jock itch spray and Rid. I was trying to kill Daddy, not cure jock itch or kill any crabs. As I was walking out of Tonio's room, I saw what looked to be several pages torn out of Mama's notebook. What did he have to do with all of this? Was he in on these dysfunctional ass family values, too? No, not Antonio. I loved him, and he loved me, too. When I read them, they were even more heartbreaking. Mama had written stuff in there about him, too.

It read:

My Son

My son, my son, my son
I wish you never were born
To grow up and see your father treat us this way
God knows that, after all these years, I still continue to
pray
I did my best with you, all I could
I only wanted Daddy to be the man he should.
Instead, a lot of this has to do with our past.
My life cycle is a pattern that's continuing to last.
You and your sister do not deserve this mess.
One day, I'm gonna get a knife and stab daddy in the
chest
He doesn't deserve to be alive and see us smile
Knowing that we're so torn inside the whole while
God got my mama, and He'll get him, too
I just hope he gets a chance to tell you that he loves you
Waiting on God, not knowing how much of this I can
take
But I know the power of God, it's all worth the wait…
                    The End

Mama had written about Tonio, too. If he hadn't taken it, would she have given it to him? Why didn't he come to me and talk about this? Did Daddy fuck him, too? Did Mama fuck him? Did they really go to church and bingo? I was thinking all kinds of shit. The next page was balled up. I straightened it out and it was a poem called "God, Please Don't Let it be Too Late."

94

God, Please Don't Let It be Too Late

God, please don't let it be too late
I'm in this world and there's just too much hate
I don't think hate is the word I should say
I always pray to God to see another day
Women of the world, we have to step up and raise our
kids
Men, you have to help because it takes two
And plus all of our boys need a relationship with you
But, guess what? They're being raised by the streets
And being in those mean streets isn't the right place to
be
I have kids, a lot of kids, I might add,
But no one can take a place of a real dad
My five kids could be bad and out of control
But I let them know if they fuck up, there are
consequences and they slow their roll
God, I ask you again please help all the young kids
today
Some kids don't even want to go outside to play
Because they're caught up in a world of "HELL"
God, please touch their hearts before they are headed to
"HELL"
MEN! MEN! I beg of you
Being in your kids lives is the right thing to do
It seems right now that everyone is having a rough
time
But all the kids need is a little quality time
Money is the "ROOT OF ALL EVIL" or at least that's
what they say
But you're the one that has to face God on judgment
day
God does have a plan for all of our lives
All we have to do is think high and STRIVE

No one is put on this earth to be one hundred percent
But GOD will forgive us all if we just repent
Kids, it's okay for you to listen to grown-ups
sometimes
Remember they've been here longer than you. They
have a "SHARPER MIND."
Go to school until you finish school
Dropping out of school isn't cool
We all could listen and learn
And the reward will be worth the earn
If we all do right, before it's too late,
God will let all of our lives turn out just great

Too late for what?...Why didn't Mama get help?...Why didn't she leave Daddy?...Why had she stayed with him after all these years?...

Chapter Twenty-Two
Daddy's Last Nut

I put the paper back under Tonio's bed when I heard Daddy calling my name. The nerve of this sick bastard. I was seventeen years old and had been fucking him since I was twelve years old. This shit was going to stop today.

"Coming, Daddy," I said, thinking quickly that I'd just use the bleach. Fuck it. I went into the bathroom and neatly sucked some bleach into Daddy's syringe. I rinsed it off with cold water. Then, I sprayed on some of Mama's Sand & Sable perfume to help kill the odor. When I got in there with Daddy, he'd already used that vacuum pump to make his dick hard. Since Daddy was sick, he wasn't able to perform like he used to.

"What took you so long?"

"I was freshening up for you, Daddy."

I was crazy to keep fucking Daddy for all these years, but I had his blood and Mama's blood running through my veins. So, I was capable of doing anything. I just didn't give a fuck. They didn't care, and I didn't either.

"You ready, Daddy?"

"You know I am."

"You want me to ride you?"

"Yes."

I slid my shorts off and hid the syringe under the pillow as I got on top of him.

"Tonae, you keep me feeling good after all these years. You really know how to keep a man."

I was thinking I never wanted to see dick again. I started riding Daddy slow like an exotic dancer, so I could ease my hand under the pillow to get the syringe. After about 12 or 13 good hard strokes of riding Daddy, I stuck the syringe in his heart. Daddy's last words were, "What's that smell?"

I stuck that needle in his chest like I was carving a piece of wood. Daddy came at the same time he noticed the smell of bleach. Daddy had a massive heart attack. He died instantly. I kissed him on the forehead and closed his eyes.

Chapter Twenty-Three
Dealing with Daddy's Death

Mama and Tonio were saddened by Daddy's death. I really didn't know how to feel. Daddy was a human-devil. Mama, as she cried, said, "God, don't make no mistakes. He's probably in heaven with my Big Mama."

I wanted to ask her about her mama and Big Mama, but that wasn't the time. I knew she didn't believe that his ass was in heaven after all the shit he had done to me, to us. How could she have even fixed her mouth to say that? I hoped she was laughing on the inside because Daddy was her step-daddy. How would that look on his obituary? Daddy died two weeks before my graduation. He probably was gonna die soon anyway because the doctor had ordered him to stop drinking, and he didn't. I just helped speed up the process. And to help me, I had to kill him. I think I did the family a favor. Tonio had mixed feelings. I could tell he had something on his mind.

Finally, he said, "How could Daddy make you and Mama do all that shit to him when y'all were kids? How could he do it, period? Come on. Let's go to my room. I got something to show you."

He reached under the bed and got that paper and gave it to me. I acted like I was surprised. I had already read it.

"Tonae, I got this from Mama's notebook. I wanted to tell you, but I just found this last week. Mama kept a lot of secrets. How could they both be so cold-hearted?"

I interrupted him and asked if Daddy had had sex with him, too.

"NO! He never touched me. Hell. He hardly said anything to me. I wished he would have come to my basketball games."

Tears came to his eyes, and mine started to water, too. He showed me some more papers that Mama had recently written about my junior high teacher, Mrs. Lawrence:

I know she's fucking him.
Tonae's teacher. She was always in my face at bingo.
I knew something was going on because when he first got sick
She was crying more than I was.
She used to visit him at Crawford Long Hospital
When I was at work, she used to bring his favorite pop by the house.
She'd call to try and catch his voice to answer the phone.
Instead of hanging up, she'd play it off and talk about Tonae's grades.
I've been stupid for all these years.
I was letting my step-daddy, who was my husband, sleep with my only precious daughter.
Damn you, Mama, for this curse you have on me.
And damn you, Big Mama, you could have saved me.
God, what have I done?
I don't even know how to love the only two kids that you've given me.
The End

We both were crying.

He said, "Sis, I had no idea. I would have killed Daddy myself. Good thing he had that heart attack because he would have had a lot of explaining to do."

Tonio had no idea that I killed Daddy. If he was alive, he wouldn't have wanted to hear his weak ass explanation.

"Tonae, and Mama? What kind of person is she? She allowed all of this to happen to you. She didn't do nothing."

"Tonio, Mama only knew what she knew and that was to do as her Mama had done. Tonio, I'm almost grown now, and I forgive Mama. I don't know why, but I do. I don't know why this happened to us, but it did. I have no answers either. I do know Mama has love inside of her for us, and she doesn't know how to let it out. Tonio, Mama was very young. Did you read the part in her journal about her mama wanting her to have a baby for her? That baby turned out to be me."

"Yes, I did, and where is she? I'd like to tell her how she fucked this family up."

"She's dead. Tonio, we have to be strong for each other."

Tonio said that he was joining the army next year when he graduated.

I kissed him on the cheek and left his room.

Chapter Twenty-Four
Heaven Ain't No Place for My Daddy

Looking at Daddy in his casket, I saw that he didn't look shit like Bobby Knight.

Just looking at Daddy, I couldn't cry at all. The only thing that kept flashing in my head were all those grown-up games I had played with him. Daddy had always told me to just act normal. Well, that was kind of hard because I was only twelve and fucking him. He was especially cold-hearted when I used to be on my period. I was glad he was dead. I looked around, and Mrs. Lawrence had the nerve to be there in the back, crying like she had been married to Daddy. Mama was crying, too. Her nose was red. I don't know why she was crying. I fucked him more than she ever did. I should have been the one crying, but my heart wouldn't let me. My brother, Tonio, was just in a daze. He didn't cry either. I just couldn't imagine what all was racing through his head. Uncle Buck was crying, but I bet he was crying because he couldn't come over to the house to drink Daddy's favorite pop any more. Uncle Buck stopped having sex with me when I was about 13. He was supposedly in the church now. That still didn't matter. I had already prayed to God that he would die and go to hell with Daddy. I couldn't put Mr. Antonio Charles Watson, Sr. in heaven or hell.

"Let's just hope that, before he left this world, he got on his knees to repent," Pastor Riley said.

The only time Daddy got on his knees was to eat my pussy or grab his favorite pop from under the bed. Daddy hadn't gone back to church at all. I don't think he ever went. He didn't have no godly ways in his heart. Pastor Riley hadn't seen or talked to Daddy. He could only preach his funeral. Daddy was fucking before he left this world. He didn't have time to repent. He was too busy fucking me and my teacher, Mrs. Lawrence. Heaven wasn't any place for Daddy. He went straight to hell. He didn't even stop at go.

When the funeral was over. I looked back where Mrs. Lawrence was sitting, and she'd already left. Now that Daddy was dead, I could focus on graduating and going to college. Mama didn't say much on the ride home after Daddy's funeral. She wouldn't stop saying, "What am I gonna do now?"

She only worked part-time downtown. If she wanted to keep the house, she'd have to get another job. I wanted to work at McDonald's when I graduated, so I could eat all the cheeseburgers I wanted. Tonio was going to the army. I was frightened for him to go. What if he had to go to war? What if he died in war? All those war questions kept popping in my head; but, if he did go, he'd be a better man than Daddy...

Chapter Twenty-Five
Mama's Two Jobs

A week after Daddy's funeral, Mama had gotten another job at Georgia Pacific. She cleaned the offices at night. It still wasn't enough money to keep the house. Mama found out that Daddy's life insurance was only enough to pay for the funeral. She wasn't even listed as a beneficiary. No one was. My name should have been on there three or four times, considering what all I had been through with Daddy. We lost our house. We had to move to the Englewood Manor Projects in Atlanta, close to downtown. I still went to school in Decatur. We went from sugar to shit just like that. We couldn't even take most of our furniture. Mama only got approved for a two bedroom. Tonio and I had to share a room. He was mad, especially since he had to leave his basketball goal. It was terrible in Englewood. There was red dirt everywhere. People were always looking all in our windows. Dope boys were always gambling right in front of our door. Some mornings, they wouldn't even move. Mama had to walk around them when she left for work. In our apartment, there were roaches everywhere. Mama was a neat and clean person, but those roaches still took over. One time, I went in the kitchen to fix a bowl of Froot Loops, and the box was covered with roaches. Mama had to keep most of our cereals in the

refrigerator covered in plastic bags. Tonio wasn't ever there. He used to catch the bus to our old neighborhood.

"Mama, you know I'm going to be a famous singer one day."

She looked at me and said, "Finish college first."

Mama told Tonio and I not to get involved with them people over there. Tonio didn't get in any trouble because he wanted to join the army. I only had to live with them roaches for a short period of time because I soon moved on to my college's campus. The only time I ever really went outside was to dump the trash. When I did, I felt all eyes on me, especially those girls. They watched me like hawks, like I wanted their ghetto boys. Little did they know, I was done with dick. It could have been them I was looking at them. I had to thank Daddy and Uncle Buck for that. They were supposed to protect me, instead they had other plans. Bobby would have been my man, but he betrayed me for Shelia Jones. She wasn't my rival anymore. I still wanted to be with her. I hoped to see her when I became famous. One day, I would be a famous singer. I was going to get Mama out of that roach motel. I wondered where Bobby Knight was. I wondered if he was still cute. I wondered if he still went with Shelia Jones. I really did have a soft spot in my heart for Shelia.

Chapter Twenty-Six
My Graduation

I graduated from Towers High with a 4.0 GPA. I was also glad that I had gotten accepted to Clark Atlanta. Mama didn't come to my graduation, but Tonio was there. They played Whitney Houston's "The Greatest Love of All." It was nice. I was ready to get home and find Mama's notebook. She was at her night job. I caught the bus home, and Tonio went to our old neighborhood. Mama and I never really had a relationship. I still wanted to read some more of Mama's notebook. When I got home, I took off my dress and looked for Mama's notebook. I found a new one with poems Mama had written the night before.

Listen

Listen is a thing that I should have done.
Now this life that I go through is not fun.
Doing what I gotta do to get by.
If I don't find God, my soul will surely fry.
I know the right way and how to find God,
But, on this earth, I feel that the devil has won.
I am smart and you can bet your ass
When I get to the golden gates, I wanna pass.
I did shit and it's too late to take back.
My hard headed ass, I just wish God would smack.
He showed me signs that I ignored,
But it was my heart that he'd poured.
I was a fool, and it's out of sight.
A second chance, huh? He just might.
Drinking and getting high won't solve a thing.
When it's my mind, body, and soul to Jesus I should
bring.
If I die tonight, because of my health,
Sorry, kids, there was no insurance money left.

Love

Love is a word that I just heard
Come on. Let's keep it real. Love is absurd.
All this shit that is going on today.
Love should have taken a toll and got in the way
We always say that God don't make mistakes,
But what about the bastards who take lives away?
I'm gonna die, and it's okay
Just long as I know my maker, I'll see one day.
I pray and pray, and it seems I continue to frown,
But never knew that God was always around.
So just because God is here in spirit,
I need to listen and quit pretending not to hear it.
He loves me and loves you and this I know.
If we don't straighten up, the opposite of heaven is
Where our souls will go.
It was His decision. He already made.
Thinking we're getting away with shit,
It was ourselves that we played!!!!

Mother, Mother

Mother, Mother
Where are you, Mother?
Please stop acting undiscovered.
You're here nor there.
Instead, you're everywhere.
I think of you all the time
I just can't seem to get you off my mind.
I love watching pictures of you,
But I can't accept the fact that our
Mother/daughter relationship is through.
I love you very, very much,
But I can't meet you halfway if you don't keep in touch.
I won't talk much about your past.
I just want our friendship to last.
I've already forgiven you and the things you've done.
Mom, I just want to see you and move on!!!!!

Chapter Twenty-Seven
Tonio's Going to the Army

Tonio looked so handsome in his tuxedo. His graduation was nice. He didn't look like Daddy at all. He looked like a model. I was glad that he finished school. Mama didn't make it to his graduation either. but she did drop him off at Fort Gillem. I stayed at home, so I could read some more of her journal. I kissed Tonio and gave him the biggest hug and told him to write me the first chance he got. The only daddy Tonio ever had was Dr. Huxtable from *The Cosby Show*. I wished I was a part of their family. They had good family values, but my life, as a child, wasn't shit like Rudy's. Claire really had her family in order. Unlike Mama, she cared. Maybe, once I became famous, we all could get some professional counseling. Mama was so hurt. I could tell by her journal. Maybe Dr. Phil could straighten our family out. Hell. Maybe even Oprah. I loved Oprah. I wanted to meet her one day. She was such a generous person, saving the world and all. Antonio didn't seem like he had butterflies. Although he had gotten a basketball scholarship to go to Georgia Tech, he turned it down and went to the army. Antonio was on his way to becoming a real man. I was going to college to major in English and Fine Art. I felt sorry for Mama. When they left to go to Fort Gillem, I went to find that notebook. Mama had more poems.

God, I Quit

God, I quit. I know it don't sound true.
Truth be told. I wanna get closer to you.
Yes, I screwed up, and this I know,
But I'm tired of hearing "I told you so".
I've asked this question over and over, so
"Please, don't let it be too late".
I know it won't be if I continue to have faith and pray.
Doing this self-destruction out of spite
Is doing nothing but quickly ending my life.
Oh God, Oh God, hear me now.
I wanna do right and just don't know how.
Year after year, being stoned
How can I tell my beautiful kids that I've been so wrong?
They deserve a good mother, and I will do my best.
God, if I put forth an effort, can U please do the rest?

Finally Free

How the fuck your ass gonna hit me in the head with a gun
When I was 6 months pregnant with our son?
Caught your stupid ass cheating late at night.
You get mad at me and start a fight.
Ol' girl looking at me like I'm wrong
When she's the one that broke up our so-called happy home.
The more and more I think about that shit
Your head is the one that should have been split.
You had the up on me because you was a man.
Being in a relationship with you was the wrong plan.
Caught you cheating red handed and I took your ass back
Knowing I should have left your ass where I found you at
I'm raising our son to never hit a girl.
Once he has your evil ways will be the end of his world.
Why did you have to beat me, turning me black and blue
When you knew deep down inside how much I loved you?
I heard that you beat all your other women after me.
I'm just glad I'm done with your ass and finally free.

Before Birth

Hello, how are you?
You mean to tell me I'm about to be through.
I'm just a little one in here.
I just wanna see you and be near
Your warm heartbeat and touch.
Mom, if you keep me, I promise you'll be loved so much.
You're too young and that's okay.
Just remember that God always makes a way.
Life is hard, and, yes, you're strong.
Make the right decision. Don't do wrong.
Just let me make it, and you will see
That I might not turn out as bad as you thought I'd be.
I feel a pinch, and, yes, it do hurt.
Mom, please don't put me in the dirt.
That was hard, but, where I'm at, I'm okay.
Heaven is nice, and, upon your decision,
I hope you make it here someday.

Life After Death

There is life after death. Believe it or not.
The rate I'm going my eternal life will be hot.
Knowing what's right and continuing to do wrong
Will always have a disturbing home.
Telling my kids one thing and doing another.
God, how much longer can I be undercover?
This life I'm taking right now for a joke
Will not be funny at the end without no hope.
I don't know when it'll be over and that's for sure,
But dwelling this earth I can no longer endure.
I need to get it together and make a change
Now watch all my so-called friends say that I'm acting
strange.
I wanna do right, and it isn't for show.
When I leave this world heaven is where I wanna go.

Chapter Twenty-Eight
College Finally

A week after Tonio left for the army, I went off to college. I was ready to leave, too. I was tired of hearing gun shots in Englewood. Mama would be living there all alone. I thought Mama would have peace of mind once we were gone. She had all the time in the world to think about how she could love us. She could also think about how she had let Daddy fuck me, instead of her. I was packing my things and thinking about Shelia Jones. I'd been thinking about her for the last 5 years. I really wanted to see her. Bobby Knight? Well, I could care less. He was probably somewhere getting his dick sucked at our old school yard.

Mama drove me to Clark Atlanta University. The school was brown with white trimmings and had the school's name in front in big bold black letters. I kissed Mama good-bye and went inside. It was crazy packed. There were students everywhere. I glanced around, and I saw them divided in groups. There was your rich black girl group, some with fake blonde hair that reminded me of Daddy's porn. There were dread head black boys. Prep boys. I didn't fall in any one of those categories.

I went to the dorm they assigned me on my registration paper. When I got there, a girl was already in there unpacking her things. I sat my stuff on the floor and laid on the bed. I noticed a rainbow flag was hung

115

on her side of the room. Classes didn't start until the next day. I had all night to put my things up. I glanced at her. She was about 5'6 with a pretty shape. She had curly black hair. And her complexion was a shade darker than mine. I wondered if she had a boyfriend. I didn't want a boyfriend. I wanted clit, not dick. I wondered if she was bi-sexual or straight.

I was officially gay. I didn't want another man to ever touch me. Daddy made it clear that he was the only man for me. Daddy was supposed to protect me. I stressed that because all my friends' daddies had been their protectors, but my daddy made me his toy that he played with anytime he felt like it. Uncle Buck was a complete asshole. I didn't even cry when Mama told me that he had died in a car wreck. I thought, Good for him. I knew he was in hell. Now, he and Daddy could play those stupid grown-up games together. I hoped the devil had put them in a pool of burning water.

Enough reminiscing. If I kept thinking about my past, I wouldn't be able to get through college. I had made it this far by the grace of God.

Now, back to this hot chick I was sharing the dorm with. I wondered if she had kids? I wondered what her name was? I would have had kids if Mama wouldn't have taken me to get that wash out. My child would have been five years old. It was a good thing she took me to that clinic because Mama would have been my child's step-mom and grandma. Damn. There I went having flashbacks again.

I finally said, "Hi, I'm Tonae. What's your name?"

"Who? Me?"

"Yes. Who else is in this room?"

"I'm Amber. Amber Cooper."

As she talked, I noticed that she had on a rainbow necklace and bracelet. I thought she could definitely be

on TV with that smile. She had a set of teeth that were fit for a Colgate commercial. She was from Riverdale, GA. She said her first choice was to go to Clayton State College, but her mom wanted her to be closer to her. Her mom lived in a loft on Northside Drive. She was definitely my type. She talked a lot, but I liked that. That let me know that she was a good listener. I wanted to ask her if she had a man, but I didn't know how to do it just yet.

I asked, "Does this college have talent shows?"

"Oh, I don't know. Well, Miss Tonae, since I've told you about me, tell me about you."

"I'm from Decatur." I was about to tell her that we lost our house and had to move to the ghetto, instead I said, "I have brother who is in the army. I'm majoring in English and Arts, but my true dream is to become a famous singer one day."

"Oh, so you can sing?"

"Yes, just like Patti LaBelle."

"Well, I just happen to be going to this bar tonight that has karaoke. Since you're my roommate, let's hang."

Chapter Twenty-Nine
Singing Karaoke

We left in Amber's car. She had a black Lexus coupe. I knew that when I became famous, I'd be able to buy any car I wanted. Amber had on a black dress with a rainbow belt and rainbow accessories to match. That dress hugged every inch of her body. I also had on a black body dress. I had gotten thicker over the years. I was about 5'3 and looking good. I had on a pair of leather thigh boots. We were going to a sports bar in Jonesboro. I had no idea where that was. All I knew was Decatur— where it's greater. She said the food there would be absolutely delicious. I wasn't hungry because I had eaten some of Mama's good spaghetti. I followed Amber to the front to sign up. She knew the place because it was her neck of the woods. After that, we took a table by the stage.

"What can I get you guys?" the waiter asked.

"I'll have a shot of Jack Daniels on the rocks," Amber answered.

"And for you, ma'am?"

"I'll have one, too. Thanks," I said to the waiter. As the waiter left, I turned to Amber and asked, "You drink Jack Daniels?"

"My granddaddy used to drink that everyday all day before he died."

"His name wouldn't happen to be Antonio Watson, would it?" I joked.

"No, silly. His name was Albert Martin Cooper, the third."

We definitely had chemistry. We got our drinks. I smelled hers to make sure it wasn't watered down.

"Can we buy you two ladies a drink?" asked this guy as he and his partner helped themselves to our table.

One was white with slick black hair, and the other was a black boy with a nice hair cut with about twenty gold teeth. He didn't say anything. He just smiled. I was cracking up on the inside because when he did say something his top grill moved.

"No, you can't," Amber snapped, "Do you not see the rainbow gear I have on? Do you even know what it means?"

Those guys didn't even have time to answer her.

She said, "We're gay. This is my girlfriend."

I almost choked on my drink. They apologized and went to the next ladies they saw.

"Gay? Amber, you're gay?"

"Yes. Do you have a problem with it?" she snapped.

"No, of course not."

I waved for the waiter to bring me another drink.

That explained the rainbow flag she had hanging in our room. She was gay and proud. I knew I had seen that rainbow on CNN when Ellen Degeneres's show got cancelled when she came out the closet. People had threatened to blow up ABC's studios, but as more people came out of the closet, the less it became a major issue. I loved Ellen. She was funny.

119

"So, how long have you been gay, Amber?"

"Since I was 13. I just never really had no type of attraction to boys. I've always liked pretty girls such as yourself. What about you?"

"Me, too," I lied.

I wasn't about to tell her that my daddy had fucked me gay, so I went along with her reason. It sounded a lot better than mine.

"So, you got anymore rainbow stuff?"

"Yes, I do. I have a lot."

I wanted some, so I could handle guys like Amber had just handled those two jocks.

"When we get back, I can give you a cute little rainbow ring. So, Miss Tonae, do you have a girlfriend?"

"No, but I want one."

"Well, consider yourself taken because I'm looking, too."

"Sounds nice to me."

The show was about to start. The first man sang "All Night Long" by Lionel Ritchie, but his voice didn't go with his looks. He sounded like Jeffrey Osborne or Billy Ocean. I had finished two drinks and decided not to have another one. When they called my name, I wasn't even nervous because I had been performing in front of people ever since I was six years old.

"Go get 'em, baby," Amber said.

That sounded good coming from her.

When I got to the stage, I didn't need a monitor. I knew all of Patti songs. My song was "If You Ask Me To." I cleared my throat and sort of looked at the crowd. I saw a man with a big gold chain on in the second row. He was writing in a notepad. I didn't know if he was in the music business or what. I began to sing. I looked at Amber, and she smiled at me. I saw that

smile all the way from the stage. I moved and sang like
Patti. I thought I was the real Patti. When it was over, I
walked by that guy with the notepad. He reached out to
introduce himself.

"Hi, I'm Mikey, and you have a superstar's
voice."

"Thanks."

"Here's my card. Please call me ASAP."

Amber got up from the table to see what was up.

She came and kissed me in front of Mikey to let
him know that I was already taken. I had never done
anything out in the open with a girl. She extended her
hand toward Mikey.

"Hi, I'm Amber, and Tonae is my girlfriend."

"Well, Amber, nice to meet you both. I was just
telling Tonae that she has a beautiful voice. You ladies
enjoy the rest of the evening."

"Amber, why did you kiss me in public?"

"You're gay, right?"

"Yes, but not quite. I mean not open like you
are."

"Oh, don't be afraid, Tonae. You'll get used to it."

We took our seats and finished watching the
show. I put Mikey's business card in my wallet. It read:
Mikey, CEO of Make It Happen Records.

"You did great," Amber said, "You do have a
beautiful voice."

"You've got a beautiful smile."

"If my smile is so beautiful, then come over here
and kiss me."

She was so pretty. I reached over and kissed her.
When I finished, I saw this man frowning at us.

"Don't worry about him. We're going to get a lot
of people judging our lifestyle. Don't you forget about
me when you blow up, Miss Tonae."

"I could never forget about you. You're the one who got me discovered if that Mikey man is who he says he is."

Amber said, "I'll drink to that."

She waved the waiter over. She ordered an amaretto sour; and, of course, I got a shot of Jack on the rocks. She took her shoes off and rubbed her feet against my legs under the table. I really liked her. I loved the attention she gave me. We finished our drinks. Amber ordered wings to go, and we left.

When we got back to the room, Amber didn't waste no time giving me that rainbow ring. She told me to wear it on my left ring finger and to never to take it off no matter what. I kinda sensed a little aggressiveness with Amber. I liked the attention she was giving me, but the way she flew up when Mikey was talking to me made me think twice. I just had to make sure I didn't hurt her in any way because there was no telling what she would do. While Amber was on her bed eating her wings, I went over to take her shoes off. She was just sexy, and she had nice legs and pretty feet, too.

"You know I want us to be together forever," Amber said.

"Me, too."

She put the wings up and motioned me to come to her. We kissed, and she said, "Let's take a shower together."

I was all new to this lifestyle, but she was definitely showing me all the ropes I needed to know. We got in the shower, and she started licking my nipples. Then, she just took charge. She didn't look like it, but she was strong. She lifted my legs up on the end of the tub and went to work on my pussy. Not only did I cum once, but I had multiple orgasms. She was licking and saying, "Whose pussy is this?"

It felt so good. I said, "Yours, Amber baby, yours."

I tried to keep my head from falling from all those shots of Jack Daniels. I wanted to do her, too, but she was like, "No, we got plenty of time for that." She just wanted me to hold her all night.

Chapter Thirty
First Semester

Amber and I were inseparable. We were like Bonnie and Clyde. When you saw me at school, you saw Amber. I wasn't ashamed of my gay lifestyle because almost everyone at school was gay or bi-sexual. One day, while we were at lunch, I had walked away to go use the restroom. Amber went to the office to have them page me over the PA system.

"Tonae! Tonae Watson! You're needed in the main office."

I thought it was news about my brother in the army. When I got to the main office, it was Amber.

"Baby, you gotta let me know before you just up and leave like that."

"Okay, Amber, I will next time."

"Better yet. Next time, you come with me when I use the bathroom."

"Okay, baby. I sure will."

Amber was obsessed with me. She had already gotten my name tattooed on the left side of her neck. It read Miss Tonae with a treble clef symbol. I wasn't even famous yet. She wanted me to get her name on me. I thought about it. I told her once I became famous I would.

One day, while Amber was testing, I wanted to go lay down, but she wanted me to stay in class with her.

I said, "Baby, I'm right down the hall. Focus on the test and not on me so much."

I went in the room to lay down. I was asleep until I was awakened by Amber rubbing on my clit.

"Wake up, sleepy head. I'm back."

She used her tongue to lick me everywhere. She put some whip cream on my pussy and licked it.

Just when I was about to cum, she stopped and put a silver bullet on my clit to finish the job. Damn, I didn't care if this girl was crazy. I wasn't gonna let her go. She made me feel good. She made me feel so special. She made me feel wanted. I wanted to do her, but she just wanted me to hold her. I don't know why she didn't want me to go down on her. I did wanna taste her. I wondered if I remembered how to eat pussy. I hadn't eaten anyone out since Lisa McKinney. That following week, I called Mikey.

Amber was right there.

"Hello."

"Hi. May I speak to Mikey, please?"

"This is Mikey."

"Hi, Mikey. This is Tonae. You met me—"

"I know. You're Lil' Miss Patti. I've been waiting for you to call. How are you doing?"

"I'm doing great."

Amber was licking in my ear and making my pussy wet while I talked.

"Are you busy at the moment?"

"No."

"Well, why don't you meet me for lunch? Are you familiar with Buckhead?"

"No, not really."

Amber must have heard him through the phone because she shook her head yes.

"Yes, yes. Where do you want to meet?"

"Meet me at the Brookwood Grill on Peachtree Street at 3 PM."

When we got there, Amber walked me in and spoke to Mikey. He was sitting in the bar with a lady. A pretty lady, I might add. Amber kissed me in front of them and told me to call her when I was ready. He introduced me to his lady friend.

"Tasty, this is Tonae, the lady I've been telling you about."

She sure did look tasty, too.

"So, Miss Tonae, Do you have any songs, yet?"

"Well, actually. I do have a few. They are called "Stop Cheating on Me," "You're Only a Substitute," and "Grow.""

He said, "When will you be ready to go to the studio?"

"I'm ready now."

"You can ride with us."

I probably should have called Amber to let her know before she called Channel 5 and reported me missing. We rode in his Lexus ES400. We got to the studio, which was in the West End, not too far from school. I walked in, and it was already crowded with different artists. They was smoking and drinking, but we walked through all that and went to his main studio, which was upstairs. Immediately, we started working on my album.

The name of my album was called *Don't Dislike it, Get Like It.* Mikey had some nice beats, and he also had some more songs. We stopped, and he told me to meet him back there at 8 AM sharp the next day. He dropped me off at the school. I walked in, and Amber was asleep with her face in her book and her pen in her hand. I moved the book and the pen.

"Did you call me? I'm sorry," she said as she woke up and wiped her face.

"No, I didn't call, baby. We went to the studio to work on some songs, and the studio just happens to be right up the street in the West End."

"Well, how did it go?"

"It went well. I need you to drop me off at the studio in the morning at 8 AM."

"Who was that lady he was with?"

"Oh, her name is Tasty. She's one of his artists."

"Tasty?"

"Yes."

"Well, did Tasty get at you?"

"No, baby. Not every woman wants me. Amber baby, don't worry. I'm true to you," I said, raising up my hand and showing her that ring she had given me.

She smiled and said, "I love you, and I want us to be together forever."

"I love you, too."

I really wasn't too focused on that college work because I had gotten the green light from Mikey that I was going to record my album. On the other hand, Amber kept herself busy with work while I was at the studio.

Chapter Thirty-One
The Real Amber

As time went on, Mama still worked two jobs. Mama told me that Tonio was learning good discipline in the army. I knew Tonio could handle himself in there because he didn't get in any trouble. He was always playing basketball or his video game. Tonio didn't even go to our junior high prom. Tonio had had a couple girlfriends in high school, but they weren't anything serious. One time, Tonio had this girl by the name of Stacey Burns in the garage. It was right after school. I was usually down at Bobby Knight's house, but not on this day. I came home to find my cut-up jeans that were stored out there. I was getting ready for an up-coming talent show. Lisa was going to be with me in the talent show. We were going to be Salt-N- Pepa and perform the song "Push It."

Anyway, when I opened the garage, I heard some moaning and groaning. Tonio was on top of an old dryer that had burned out. And Stacy was on her knees sucking his dick. I walked in and wasn't even shocked. I had seen so much of that already with Daddy.

Tonio said, "What are you doing home?"

Stacey jumped up, wiping the thick white stuff from her mouth.

I said, "Boy, you ain't got nothing I ain't ever seen before."

I went back in the house to wait 'til they were done.

A few minutes later, Tonio said, "Man, sis, you scared the shit out of us coming in the garage like that."

"I'm sorry, Tonio. I was trying to get ready for the talent show. You seen my cut-up jeans I made last summer?"

"No, I can't say that I have."

"So, was getting your rod sucked good?"

Even after all these years, I was still calling a dick a rod. When Daddy and I used to watch the porn movies on mute, the caption would come on and dick was every other word that would appear on the TV screen.

Daddy said, "The noise of them women slows up my concentration. They scream and yell for no reason. If they had my dick in them, then they'd have a reason to yell."

I hated when Daddy made comments like that. Daddy didn't even make me yell. I had gotten used to his dick. As a matter of fact, my pussy was molded to Daddy's dick. Tonio wasn't a virgin. He'd lost his virginity in the 9th grade.

"Man, sis, she was sucking my dick like she was trying to find out how to get to the middle of a tootsie pop."

Mama had given Tonio my address at school so that he could write me. Amber was still my girl. She was still dropping me off at the studio. Mikey and I were almost done with my album. The week before he had said that, once I was finished, he had a contract ready for me to sign for one million dollars. One million dollars sounded good. I could buy Mama a house, so she could leave the ghetto. When I first went to Amber's mother's house, she was out in the yard planting flowers. It was on a Saturday. It was sunny in Hotlanta. Amber looked

almost identical to her mom. In fact, they could go for sisters.

"Mom, this is my girlfriend, Miss Tonae."

Amber's mom must have already accepted Amber's gay lifestyle because she took off her right garden glove and extended her hand for me to shake.

"Hi. Nice to meet you, Miss Tonae. I'm Amber's mom, Ms. Cooper."

"Come on. Let me show you my old room," Amber said.

We entered her house. It was so big and nice. There were pictures of Amber and her previous girlfriend all throughout. Her mom must have really liked her because she had her pictures in almost every room in the house, even in the foyer. When we got to her room, it looked like Amber had just left. Her room was nice and neat. I sat on the edge of her bed, and she went to her jewelry box on her dresser. She handed me a rainbow bracelet and necklace that were almost made like hers.

"Baby, don't take this off. This symbolizes our lifestyle as well as our love for each other."

I didn't know if I loved Amber or not, but I did know she had shown and taught me some things that I didn't know. She showed me all the gay hot night spots in Atlanta. We went to the Wetbar, Atlanta Eagle, and Paris Decatur just to name a few. She was on my ass in those clubs too, especially when we went to the strip club. We went to Guys and Dolls on East Ponce de Leon. We were on my side of town then. I knew Decatur like the back of my hand. When we got there, we went to VIP. I had seen a couple of people I had gone to high school with, but no sign of Shelia. I don't know why I had expected to see her in there. I just wanted to see her that bad, but I don't think Amber would have went for

that. I couldn't even speak to another girl. Amber would be like, "Do you know her? Have you fucked her?"

Anyway, while we were in VIP, this light-skinned tall thick girl came and asked if we wanted a dance.

"No. We cool," Amber said.

I wanted that girl to dance in front of me. I didn't want to go against Amber's wishes because I did want to become famous one day. *I couldn't be known as the singer who fought with her girlfriend at the strip club.* I ordered a bottle of Jack, and Amber drank her usual—amaretto sour. A few minutes went by, and this dark skinned girl with a big ass and titties came to our table.

"Do y'all girls want a dance?"

"Yes. You can dance for my girlfriend."

I was baffled. She let the fine ass girl go by, but she stopped this ugly ass girl. I mean everything was nice from her stomach on down. The girl danced to "Shake What Your Mama Gave You" by Poison Clan. And she did have a lot to shake. I looked at the stage in front of us, and that's when I locked eyes with the first girl that had come by. She was putting on a show. She was putting pool balls in her pussy and spitting them out. I had seen women on that porn with Daddy put their fists in their pussies, but a pool ball? Damn! That was interesting to watch. I realized it was a contest when the DJ said, "Yep, this girl is the winner. Everybody give it up for Miss Tae Tae. She has won $1,000.00 for her raw uncut performance—"

"Ten dollars! That'll be $10.00!"

"Oh, okay."

I was so enthused by Tae Tae's dancing that I forgot all about the dance. Amber gave the girl $10.00. She walked away with an attitude. I didn't care. I didn't want her ugly ass to dance for me anyway.

"So, why the fuck you keep staring at the stage?"

"Amber baby, it's a show."

"Yeah, but you already had pussy in your face."

"Did you see what that girl did?"

"Yes, and I saw that you were all over her, about to drool, too."

"Man, I was just enjoying the show."

She was wrong. I wasn't drooling, but my pussy was. It was dripping wet.

"I'm ready to go."

"We haven't even finished our drinks yet."

"Fuck them drinks. Let's go, Tonae."

She was loud, and I was embarrassed.

As I went out, I saw Tae Tae out the corner of my eye. I looked her way, and she winked at me. Amber was so pissed off that she didn't even notice her as we walked out the door.

I asked Amber who the girl was in the pictures throughout her house.

"Oh, that's my ex, Katrina. I used to call her Rina."

"Why did y'all break up? Where is she?"

"She's in heaven with my granddaddy and your daddy"

Maybe your granddaddy, I thought, *My daddy is in hell. I made sure of that.*

"She died in a car wreck. Did you hear about that 13 car pile up that happened on I-285 by Greenbriar?"

"Yes, I'm sorry to hear that."

If I wasn't mistaken, that was the same car wreck Uncle Buck was in. He was probably the one who caused the wreck. He and his friend, Jack. That explained why Amber was so obsessed and overprotective of me. She was afraid that something would happen to me. Many nights, at the studio, she would sleep on the sofa while I

132

recorded for hours, singing songs over and over. I had to let her know that I could be trusted. We left her mom's house and went out to eat at Applebee's on Memorial Drive. Amber called in our food. We picked it up and went back to our dorm.

Chapter Thirty-Two
I'm Making Money Now

I was at the studio finishing up my album while Amber was at school. She stayed in her books in case this singing didn't work out, but I was going to make it work. It had been my dream ever since I was a little girl. Mikey said that he was going to put out "Stop Cheating on Me" first. It was a song about a married couple. The lady knew her husband was cheating on her. She stayed with him and prayed that he'd get over his addiction.

Stop Cheating on Me

Chorus:
Stop cheating on me
I love you and you love me
This is not how it's supposed
To be, so please, baby, stop
Cheating on me

Verse 1:
Baby, how could you do this to me?
I'm sitting home all alone and
You're out somewhere you don't belong
Please, baby, I'm begging you
Please, think and take time out and stop
Because this is not what love's about

Chorus:
Stop cheating on me
I love you and you love me
This is not how it's supposed to be
So, please, baby, stop cheating on me

Verse 2:
We've been to church and
I know we can make it
You should try harder and stop faking out
I pray about us over and over
With another person
I can't start over
Please, baby, please, give us another try
Stop the cheating and God will show you how to be
The man for me
I'll continue being the woman God made me to be

Chorus:
Stop cheating on me
I love you and you love me
This is not how it's supposed to be
So, please, baby, stop cheating on me

My single went platinum. It wasn't only on the radio. It played for commercials. The beat would play while the radio personality asked, "Are you tired of being cheated on?" I couldn't believe it. I was on the radio! I had signed a contract for one million dollars! I opened up an account and wrote checks for most of my gifts and stuff. Amber took me shopping for a car. We went to Hank Aaron BMW in Union City. I picked out a 745 BMW. It was all white with white rims. Mikey also suggested that I change my image a little. He was really talking about my hair. He wasn't talking about my

lifestyle because we were in Atlanta, the gay capital of the world. Amber knew someone who did hair on Jonesboro Road. The name of the salon was called Tammy's Exquisite Hair Salon. Tammy's salon was designed with nothing but elegance. She played soft music that made me feel right at home. The next day, we drove my car to go house shopping. We went to Buckhead. There were many nice houses out there. I didn't have to worry about Mama being too far because I was going to get her a better house, too. We saw a for sale sign while we were on Roswell Rd.

The realtor was just about to leave. I had fallen in love with this house. It was big with a circle driveway. The landscaping was to die for. All the flowers were blooming, and there were little bushes that were neatly trimmed. The realtor was a short white lady. She was just about to pop the lock on her keys to her Mercedes Benz. I hurried out the car because I didn't want her to leave.

"Hi, I'm Tonae. Is this house up for grabs?"

"Yes, it is now because I've been out here three weeks in a row getting stood up by the same person. I'm Mrs. Smith. Victoria Smith."

"I'm Tonae, and this is Amber."

By that time, Amber had already parked the car.

"Hi, I'm Amber, Tonae's girlfriend."

Amber let everyone we came in contact with know that we were lovers. The lady looked at us in confusion and then said, "Follow me. I'll show you guys the house."

She didn't look like she was older than Mama. Mama was only 45. We entered the house, and I first noticed the stairs that were divided. There were two ways you could get upstairs. Amber's house was big but not as big as this one. The great room was big. There was

already a TV screen hanging from the ceiling. She showed me the remote that controlled it and the electric fireplace. It even controlled the blinds. *So this is how they do it in Buckhead, huh?*

The carpet was so thick that our feet could sink in, and they did when we took our shoes off to enter the house. That carpet looked like a piece of heaven. We walked down the long foyer to get to the kitchen and the living room. The kitchen was so huge. There was an island in the middle and an electric range that you could put about twelve pots on. Mama would love this house.

We only had one that worked in the kitchen in Englewood. I had never ever seen a stove like that before. The appliances were all stainless steel. The refrigerator was sub-zero, which was very nice. When you opened the freezer it told the temperature!

Mrs. Smith's asking price was $350,000. Amber had wondered to the back where the pool was. I stayed with Mrs. Smith. We went to the master bedroom. It was so huge. It was the size of Mama's apartment in Englewood. The bathroom had showerheads all over the shower wall. Your whole body could get wet at one time. I looked at the rest of the house. It was just breathtaking. I asked Mrs. Smith if she knew anyone who could decorate my mom's room. I wanted everything in there to be Betty Boop. She told me that she did know someone, but she'd have to get back with me on that. Amber found us back in the kitchen. We were talking about the deeds and paperwork at that point. Amber went over it with me.

Mrs. Smith said, "They have a financing company we can go through."

Apparently, this lady didn't listen to the radio because I was all over the airwaves. She must have been

too busy to watch TV too because I was on all the video channels.

"Well, I'm sure you do have financing. You just tell me where to sign, and I'll give you a check plus a nice tip for being at the right place at the right time. I love this house, Mrs. Smith."

Amber said, "Mrs. Smith, this is Miss Tonae, the singer."

Mrs. Smith was still lost. She didn't know that she had a famous singer in her presence.

"Oh, Miss Tonae, is it?"

"Yes."

"Well, I can't say that I have heard your music. I'm so busy with my line of work."

When she found that out, she was quick to hand me the deeds to sign. She gave me the keys. We walked her out, and I handed her a CD of mine. She left with the biggest smile on her face.

We went back in the house. Amber went to the kitchen. She called me to find her. When I got there, she was on the island with no clothes. She stood on her knees, saying, "Tonae baby, come to me. Come to me."

I went over, and I laid her on her back. I kissed her. She said, "You know there is a tattoo place right up the street."

I had forgotten that I had told her that once I got famous I would get her name tattooed on me. I did have second thoughts, but she had been with me this far. I didn't even think about Daddy hardly or Shelia Jones.

I said, "Yeah, baby, I'll do it. I'll get your name."

As I was about to go downtown on her, she jumped up and said, "Let's go."

Chapter Thirty-Three
Tattoo Parlor

We got in my car. Amber drove. We went right down the street to the tattoo place. It was about 15 minutes from Mama's house on Lenox Road. When we got there, this white man who had tattoos and piercing everywhere greeted us. He looked scary. He even had skeletons tattooed on all his fingers.

"How can I help you, ladies?" With that heavy accent, all he was missing was chewing tobacco. "Yes. My girlfriend wants my name on her neck."

There she went with that girlfriend shit again. She had to let the world know. She might as well have taken out a special bulletin that flashed across the TV saying, "Amber Cooper of Riverdale and Tonae Ann Watson of Decatur are lesbian lovers."

The man gave us a book so that we could see his work. It was filled with all kinds of designs. I really liked one that had a heart that was stabbed and dripping with blood.

"No, baby. I don't like that one," said Amber.

Everything always had to be what she wanted. If I wanted water with lemon, she'd say you should just get iced tea. The man gave me a form to fill out that explained their sterile needle policy. I quickly read and signed it. She always had to say something, so we went with what she wanted. She wanted me to get Miss

Amber on the right side of my neck with a strawberry that had been bitten and dipped in cream. That shit hurt so bad. I wished I had had some of Daddy's Jack to get through.

Amber said, "The outline always hurts. The coloring and shading in are the easy parts."

I didn't care. It felt like I had a hot needle digging in my neck. It was all over in twenty minutes tops. I wrote him a check for $150.00. Amber was so glad that I had finally gotten her name on me. We had been lovers for almost two years.

My bank account was fat, and I was now seeing all my dreams come true. I bought a loft on Northside Drive, which was only minutes from the studio and Clark Atlanta.

Amber wanted to stay on campus. She didn't want to move with me because I was hardly ever home. She still called to check on me every minute it seemed. I was at the studio, on tour, or making videos, which consisted of many men having to be around me. I wasn't too fond of that, but I had to deal with it so that my videos would go with my songs. I had to quit school because I was well on my way to the top. My album release party was coming up in a couple of weeks. It was going to be at Club 12 in Buckhead on Cheshire Bridge Road. Amber went to her mother's house for her mother's Avon party. Amber said she couldn't miss it.

When I got home, the phone rang.

"Hello."

"Hi, this is Mrs. Smith. I was calling to let you know that the guy needs you to meet him at the house so he can do the Betty Boop decorations for you."

She gave me his phone number, and I met him there the next morning at six. She had already filled

him in, letting him know that I wanted Betty Boop everything. While he was there, I went up the street to Home's Furniture to furnish Mama's whole house. When I got there, people were staring at me and trying to look into my car. Once I parked and got out, I walked in with my Dihann Carroll black shades on. I entered the store and looked at the living room suits. I saw the one that would go perfect in Mama's house. It was a four piece black leather set with end tables to match. It had an area rug that matched it perfectly. I went to the front where an old white man was looking down his nose and through his glasses at me.

"The financing person is out. You'll have to come back tomorrow," he said with a nasty attitude.

What was it with these people telling me about a damn financing company? I could buy this whole store if I wanted. Just when I was about to snap, a nice looking white woman came and said, "Daddy, go in the back. I can handle it from here."

Then to me, she said, "Hi. Forgive my father. He's old and tells everyone who comes in here the same thing."

I thought it was because I was black. I took my shades off and said, "Oh, wow, I was about to say." "So, what can I help you with, Miss Tonae?" I was shocked that she knew who I was.

She continued, "I can really relate to your song 'Substitute.'"

My song "Substitute" was about a woman who was lonely and didn't have a man, so she started using vibrators and certain other sex toys.

Substitute

Chorus:
My novelty toys are your substitute
You keep leaving me to be with your mistress
And it ain't cute, and I'll say
It again, and I'll tell the world
My novelty toys are your substitute

Verse 1:
Playing with toys isn't so bad
You've left me constantly and I felt so sad
Don't knock it 'til you try it
It's only a couple of hundred to buy it
It'll never leave you home alone
The batteries are so damn strong
I don't have to worry about your sweat dripping on me or
        Your quickies that don't last
My substitute's speed can go slow, medium, or fast

Chorus:
My novelty toys are your substitute
You keep leaving me to be with your mistress
And it ain't cute and I'll say
It again and I'll tell the world
My novelty toys are your substitute

Verse 2:
When you do finally decide to come home
I'm already done
I'm glad you didn't come an hour earlier and spoil my fun
Watching several flicks helped me, too

But please know my novelty toys will always be your
substitute

Chorus:
My novelty toys are your substitute
You keep leaving me to be with your mistress
And it ain't cute and I'll say
It again and I'll tell the world
My novelty toys are your substitute

Verse 3:
I'm glad you decided to move on
Now my house can be a happy home
The stress and all the hell you put me through
I should have been found a substitute

To me, this lady didn't look like she had any problems getting a man, but I had learned that looks could be deceiving. Look at Amber's crazy ass. As the lady was talking, she glanced at my rainbow necklace then back to my face. She said, "Your eyes are so pretty."

"Thanks."

I wanted to give her a compliment, but I couldn't. I had Amber's face right in my mind, thinking she was watching me. Amber didn't even want me to look at another woman. I was surprised she hadn't called me yet. The sales lady kept flirting with me. She didn't have on nothing that had to do with the rainbow. When I didn't flirt back and only smiled, she said, "Miss Tonae, what can I help you with?"

"What's your name?"

"Tracy Huff. My family owns this furniture store."

"Well, Tracy, I was looking at that four piece black leather set that is in the front of the store. I want all

of it. The lamps, tables, rugs, everything. I also want that bedroom suit over there. I want everything over there. Who coordinated these rooms? They are nice. Whoever did this has nice taste."

"That would be me," Tracy said, smiling from ear to ear. She had a nice smile. There was something with me and people's smiles. I guess because that was the first thing I saw when I met a new person.

"I can have all of this to you tomorrow. There is a $250.00 delivery charge. How will you be paying, Miss Tonae, with cash, credit, or check?

"Check, of course."

When I was done, I had written her a check for $30,000 to furnish Mama's house. I even got a bedroom suit for Tonio when he came home. As I was about to leave, Tracy gave me her cell phone number and asked me to call her. I had to hide that card because Amber would have had a fit. When I got back to the house, Amber's car was parked in the driveway. I bet she had went by the studio first and then drove all the way out here. When I walked in, she was upstairs talking to the man who was doing Mama's room for me.

"Hey, baby."

She ran to me and gave me a wet kiss. The man almost fell off the ladder. I bet he would have loved to have seen our girl-on-girl action.

"Hey, baby. Why didn't you call?" I asked.

"I wanted to surprise you."

"I went by the studio, and Mikey said you weren't there, so I figured that this is where you'd be."

The man had done a good job. Mama's room and bathroom were Betty Boop everything. The main colors were pink and white. Betty Boop had on a two-piece bikini. Betty Boop was one fine cartoon character. The bedroom was red, white, and black. He had Betty Boop

curtains that matched. All I had to do was put the bed set on the bed when it was delivered. He even had Betty Boop wallpaper. I know it seemed like I was doing this room for a child instead of my mama; but, after reading her journal, I realized that she had loved Betty Boop just like I had loved Wonder Woman. I did not need to get Wonder Woman stuff because Daddy had given me everything when I was coming up.

When the man finished, I wrote him a check for $4,000.00. He deserved more than that because my mama's room was hooked up. Amber and I decided to stay the night because Tracy said that they would deliver the furniture at 7 AM. We stayed up talking in Mama's room about how successful I had become.

"I gotta admit. I didn't know you would be this big superstar," Amber said, "but, since you are, I'm your number one fan."

I thought that was so sweet. She came and laid her head in my lap. I was sitting up against the wall holding her. I don't even remember falling asleep.

The next morning, I was awakened by both the doorbell and the cell phone ringing. I looked at my watch. It was fifteen after eight. Amber went to the door, while I answered my phone. It was Tracy.

"Hello."

"Miss Tonae, my guys have been knocking for almost an hour now. Did you have a long night?"

"No. Not really, but I'm tired with all the projects I've got going on."

Amber came back in the room and listened to our conversation. I could tell she was ready to snap, so I quickly ended the conversation with Tracy.

"Who was that, baby?"

"Oh, that was the lady at the furniture store. You see we overslept."

I didn't have a clock for Mama's house yet. My intention was to go to Wal-mart and get a blow-up bed and a clock, but Amber and I had fallen asleep on the floor. The carpet was soft, but not soft enough for my back not to ache.

"The lady at the furniture store?"

"Yes, baby. Don't worry. She was the sales person. You know I do have to see, I mean deal, with other women in my profession."

"Yeah, like Tasty at the studio?"

"I told you Tasty is Mikey's fiancée."

"I know, baby. I just love you so much," Amber said.

I kissed her on the forehead and said, "I love you, too, baby. Now, let's go show these movers where Mama's furniture is going before they put a hole in the wall or something."

Neither one of them looked like he spoke English, but they pretty much knew where everything went. The third guy, who drove, was white. He must have been Tracy's brother. He put all the furniture downstairs that went down there. Then, he motioned the men to bring the bedroom furniture upstairs. When he came upstairs to Mama's room, his jaws dropped. He was like, "Betty Boop. My sister loves her."

I said, "My mama does, too. This is for her."

He said, "I'm Dave. Tracy's brother. You must be Miss Tonae. My sister has told me a lot about you. I listen to the radio, but I didn't hear your song until on the way over here. I heard 'Playing the Cards I've Been Dealt'. I really liked it."

I said, "Thanks."

Playing the Cards I've Been Dealt

Chorus:
All my life I've felt
I'm just playing the cards I've been dealt
Even in the heat of passion or on my knees I've felt
I've continued to play the cards I've been dealt

Verse 1:
Running around in the hood wasn't good at all
Especially being in the streets and making that hard fall
No matter how rough and tough it got
In the crowd I was always easy to spot
I'm out here being eager to learn this life
The things Daddy did to me, made him pay a price
I'm just a confused person in this world
Thinking back I had fun with a boy or a girl

Chorus:
All my life I've felt
I'm just playing the cards I've been dealt
Even in the heat of passion or on my knees, I've felt
I've continued to play the cards I've been dealt

Verse 2:
Back in the days, sleeping with anybody
Just to have a place to stay
I was constantly putting myself in danger
In the presence of so many strangers
I really wished I was raised
But no parents here, I only have God to praise
The things Daddy did to me was wrong
But thanks to you, Daddy, I'm so strong
If I could make a change
Your heart is what I would have changed

But looking back at everything
And considering the facts
I was just playing the cards I've been dealt

Chorus:
All my life I've felt
I'm just playing the cards I've been dealt
Even in the heat of passion or on my knees, I've felt
I've continued to play the cards I've been dealt

I thought, *What could Tracy tell him about me?* It's a good thing Amber had stepped out.

"What did your sister say about me?"

"She said that she respected you because you wear your rainbow, and you're not ashamed. Tracy is gay, but she is ashamed to be seen in public wearing the rainbow," he said as he walked to Mama's bathroom. "This is quite some work you got done. Who did this?"

"*If I tell you, I gotta kill you,*" I joked. He smiled, and I could see the resemblance. That was why Tracy was flirting with me. I didn't want this to be a magnet for every gay person in the world to notice me. Maybe Tracy just wanted to be friends. Either way, I was going to call her and find out. Once the movers were done, I gave them a $50.00 tip each. There were 5 of them, including Dave.

Amber had put Mama's bed together. We laid on the bed. It was so soft.

"Baby, when will I meet your mama?" Amber asked.

"We're going to bring her to her new house today."

"I really love you for doing all this for your mama."

Amber just didn't know all the shit I went through to get this far. We got in my car and headed to Mama's apartment.

Chapter Thirty-Four
Let's Go, Mama

We got to my mama's house and had to damn near blow the horn several times to get by. People were all in the street. Babies were in the street, holding bottles and wearing pampers and no shirts. Two buildings down from Mama's apartment, there were a lot of police surrounding the building. I bet they were looking for Big C. He was the neighborhood drug dealer. They didn't get him though. He had already left. We parked and went inside. I knocked on the door. Mama came to the door with an Englewood Manor t-shirt on. My mama had lived over there for two years. She was still pretty. I told my mama that Amber was my girlfriend. Mama understood right off the bat why I was gay. Amber didn't have to blurt out to my mama, "Hi, I'm Amber, Tonae's girlfriend."

She had more sense than that. When she saw Mama, she said, "Wow, y'all look like sisters."

I hugged Mama. She looked at Amber and asked, "How are you?"

"I'm fine."

"I love your daughter. Thanks for having her."

I begged to differ. I was one daughter who had went through hell and back.

Mama asked if we wanted something to eat. I was like hell no. I didn't want to be crunching on cooked

150

roaches. Mama had cooked neckbones, rice, and cornbread.

"No, Mama. We're fine."

I walked over to the window to look at my car. I had seen little kids putting their fingerprints all on my windows and shit.

I said "Mama, let's go for a ride. I haven't talked to you since my album dropped. We are going out to eat. You don't need nothing but your purse. We'll be back," I lied.

When we walked to my car, the kids scattered away from it like roaches do when you turn on the lights. Amber unlocked the doors, and we got in my car. It was full of fingerprints. I was pissed off. We went to the car wash down the street and got the car cleaned. While at the car wash, I saw Big C up there. He was in his old Delta 88 with tinted windows. He just tapped the horn, but not too loud, just loud enough to speak. Mama waved, too. I didn't know she knew him. I used to see him serving junkies when I used to catch the bus to school some mornings. He was a tall dude with braids. His nose was always running. Maybe he was doing more than selling drugs.

We pulled up the driveway of the new house.

"This ain't nowhere to eat," Mama said.

I said, "Mama, I know. Let's just go in here."

Mama didn't know what to think. We walked in. Mama's house looked like it belonged on *Lifestyles of the Rich and Famous*. I opened the door and took Mama upstairs to her room. Once she saw Betty Boop, she just started crying.

"Mama, you don't have to cry."

"Tonae, how did you know?"

"Mama, I read your journals. Just like I loved Wonder Woman, I read how much you liked Betty Boop."

Mama and I just broke down crying. Amber stepped out of the room. As she walked out, she had tears in her eyes, too.

"Mama I dropped out of college. It's been about two years now. I did go at first, but Amber and I went to a karaoke bar, and I got discovered by a famous producer. Mama, I have songs that are playing on the radio."

"Tonae, I never doubted you. I just wanted you to be better than me."

"I know. Mama, this is your house. You don't have to work anymore. I really think we need to get some counseling."

Mama went on asking how much of her journal I had read.

"I read enough to know that my daddy was your step-daddy. Enough to know that my daddy did the same things to you that he did to me. Mama, why didn't you leave him?"

"Tonae, I was young. My mother had a master plan that fucked my life up."

"No, it didn't, Mama. We still have each other. All that stuff Daddy did to us only made us stronger. And look at me, I've always told you I was going to be famous one day."

"Where was I gonna go? I was only twelve. All I knew was your daddy and Mama. I didn't even see Big Mama anymore. Tonae, you was my little angel. Your daddy had threatened to kill you and me if I ever left him. He got me hooked on drugs. Then, when I wanted more, he would get mad and fight me. I think your

daddy loved us, but he loved us in the wrong kind of way."

"Mama, Daddy couldn't have loved us. He made us do all that stuff to him."

"Well, baby, that's why he had to answer to God."

I wondered if I should tell Mama that I was the one who had killed Daddy.

"Mama, what Daddy did made me who I am today. If you wouldn't have been his step-daughter, then Tonio and I wouldn't be here. I can't be mad either way. Maybe one day, but definitely not today."

Knock. Knock.

"Can I come in?" Amber asked.

"Yeah, sure. Open the door."

Mama and I were done crying but not done talking. We needed to get counseling. Amber walked in and hugged Mama, who was still teary eyed.

"Ms. Watson, it'll all work out," Amber said as she continued to hug her. Amber really was a sweet person. I gave Mama the keys to the house.

"Thanks, baby. I love you so much."

"I love you, too."

Amber and I left. She jumped in her car and followed me to my loft.

Chapter Thirty-Five
Mama, Try to Forget About Daddy

It was summer, and Amber was out of school. Mama had called and left a message for me to call her.

"Hello, Mama."

"Tonae, I need to go to Englewood to get my wedding picture and all my notebooks."

I knew why she wanted her notebooks, but I didn't understand why she wanted that picture. Mama needed to forget about Daddy and let him burn in hell like he had been doing for the past three years.

"Okay, Mama, I'll be there shortly."

As I got in the shower, I heard the doorbell ring. It was Amber. She was getting prettier by the minute.

"Hey, baby."

"Hi," I said as I kissed her on her sexy lips.

She was the type of girl who didn't need any make-up. She helped herself in the kitchen while I took a shower. I was in the shower thinking about her. She didn't even call. She just came over. I was glad she was staying on campus. If she had stayed with me, I wouldn't have been able to call Tracy or have no friends. Amber was always popping up like Jason in *Friday the Thirteenth*. I remember one time when she thought I wasn't home and went to the front office to have the people unlock the door to see if I was I dead or something. I was at the gym on the third floor.

154

I got out the shower and put on my pink and gray Nike sweatsuit with my pink and gray Nike Air Max sneakers. I put my hair in a ponytail and put on my Gucci shades.

"So what are we doing today, baby?"

I wanted some space from Amber. There was something not right with her. She crowded me. She was always asking me if anyone had asked about my tattoo. She had asked if I would get her name while we were in the midst of making love. She'd already gotten my name. I didn't tell her to get my name on her.

"Well, I gotta go over to Mama's, pick her up, and take her to Englewood."

Once I said Englewood, I knew Amber wouldn't wanna go. She was scared as hell last time.

"Well, baby, call me when you get back, so we can hang out tonight."

She kissed me and left. I was glad she didn't want to go with me. I could ride in peace and listen to Sade. I liked my music, but there was something about Sade. Her music always took me away. I got in my car, jumped on the interstate, and headed to Mama's house. While on the way, I thought about Tracy. I wanted to get to know her. It had been almost a month, and I still had her phone number. I hadn't been able to call because Amber was always around, and I mean always around. One time, when I was at home talking to Mikey, I heard Amber pick up the other phone, so she could listen to our conversation.

I got to Mama's house. I had my own set of keys, so I walked in. Mama was cooking as usual. Mama was happy. She was in there listening to Betty Wright's "Clean Up Woman." Mama was sipping on some wine that Amber and I had left in there last week. Mama was feeling good. I could tell that she was happy. She turned

155

her pots off and muted the stereo until we got back. We locked up the house and headed to Englewood.

Chapter Thirty-Six
Mama, Leave it All Behind

When we got to Mother's house, she grabbed her and Daddy's wedding picture. If it had been left up to me, I would have burned it. For some reason, I didn't have any grudges against Mama because, by reading her journal, I realized we had gone through the same shit with Daddy. I loved Mama though, no matter what. I was ready to get back to Mama's house, because I wanted to call Tracy. Mama was trying to get a painting off the wall. I begged her to leave it. I knew it was filled with roaches. I told her we could find a better Picasso painting in the art store. It was a big colorful drawing of a lady reading a book with a red teardrop in her left eye. I assured Mama we'd find something similar. I didn't want her to bring any roaches to her big house. She grabbed the rest of her belongings, and we headed to the car. Like always, the kids were all around my car, amazed by the rims and the auto start. I had to go to the car wash once again because they had gotten fingerprints all over the car. I thought I was going to see Big C, but I didn't. I saw a white Bentley, though. The person driving it looked very familiar. He looked like Bobby Knight. Damn, that was Bobby. He blew the horn, got out, and whispered something to Mama.

He looked at me and said, "Damn, girl. All that dick I was giving you, how the hell you turn out gay?" I

just ignored him because I had things going for me now. Mama looked dumbfounded when I asked her what Bobby had whispered in her ear. She made up a quick lie about how she owed him money for fixing something in her old raggedy ass apartment. Even I knew there was nothing in there worth fixing, so I continued to get my car detailed. When we got back to Mama's house, I went to the guest bedroom and called Tracy. Amber was at her mom's Avon party, so I had time to see Tracy. When I called Tracy, she went on and on about how she didn't want to come between a healthy, happy relationship. My main objective was to get her over to Mama's so we could talk and possibly have sex. I really wanted to get to know her, especially since she was in the life.

I got up to take a shower. In case anything sexual did happen, I'd be ready. When Tracy got there, she looked like she was going to a job interview.

I said, "Girl, you don't have any regular clothes, do you?

She said, "I love to dress business casual."

We bypassed Mama in the front room on our way to my room. She was too busy writing in that damn journal. I had thought that since Daddy was dead all the secrets were dead, too; but I guess not. When we got in my room, we both sat on the bed. I turned on the TV. I didn't want to watch TV. I wanted to watch her get naked. Something in me started to act like Daddy. I said, "So, Tracy, tell me about you. How long has your family owned that furniture store?"

She said that she was only there that weekend to help out because her brother, Dave, had been on vacation. She was actually a lawyer with her own practice. I wanted to ask her if she wanted to play a game, but Tracy was an older woman. She didn't want to play any mind games. That was Daddy's and Uncle

158

Buck's bullshit. We just continued to talk and smile at each other. She had a smile to die for. I thought about calling Amber, but she was helping her mom. I felt strange because I'd never been in the company of another woman. I used to dream about Daddy's porn. All those women's pussies were shaved and pink. I wondered if that was the case with Tracy. I was just about to get up and close the blinds when I saw Amber staring me in the face.

Chapter Thirty-Seven
I Should Have Called Amber

Amber had been looking at us through my bedroom window at Mama's house. I couldn't believe that Amber didn't trust me even though I had thought of being with other women. I never wondered what it was like to be with a man again. Daddy made sure I wouldn't ever be with another man. He was dead and still haunting me from the grave.

When I went to open the door, I had never seen Amber look the way she did. Tracy didn't know what to think. I told her to leave and that I would call her tomorrow. Tracy ran to her car! I thought Amber was going to grab her ass! Amber and I went into my room. I was scared. I didn't know what to say. I wasn't used to this type of treatment in a relationship. The words I wanted to say didn't come out my mouth, so I started sounding like my daddy saying, "Let's have a drink, so you can calm down."

Right before Daddy and I would have sex, he'd always give me a shot of Jack Daniels. Amber wasn't going for that shot shit. She kept saying, "I thought you loved me, and I catch your ass over here with some white bitch!"

160

Would it have made a difference if Tracy would have been black? If I would have said that it would have only pissed her off even more.

"Tonae, I thought we was going to be together forever," Amber said.

"We are, but you have to let me have friends. Tracy and I were just talking."

"Well, why didn't you invite me to dinner?"

I wanted to say because your ass was always under me – at the studio, at the gym, and sometimes, when I'm shitting, you're right there holding the air freshener. What was with her and her obsession? I couldn't deal with it anymore.

"Amber baby, I am an artist. I have friends. Tracy was helping me with my next album cover."

That lie didn't work because I had already told her that Tracy was the one giving us a wake-up call the day the furniture arrived at Mama's house. Amber told me she was tired of my shit and stormed out the door saying, "You'll be sorry for hurting me!"

I wanted to run after her, but she was too upset. I figured she'd cool off and call me back. I didn't know if Tracy would still be a friend after that night. She was just as scared of Amber as I was. Amber's eyes had fire in them. All she was missing was a pitchfork in her hand because she looked like one of Satan's helpers.

Mama came in to see if I was alright. I said, "Mama, Amber thinks there is something between Tracy and I."

Mama told me that I couldn't have two women at one time. I didn't see why not. *I had Daddy and Uncle Buck all the time.* Mama told me that I needed to tell Amber that I wanted to have friends and that we needed some space. That was it – space. I was going to tell her that the next day. Mama understood my sexual

161

preference. After all, what could she say? She was one of the reasons why I chose to take that route.

Mama said that she didn't want anything to happen to me. I told Mama that Amber was looking at us through the window. Mama couldn't believe that Amber was stalking us. She made that very clear by looking through the window and not knocking on the door. Mama went back into her room. Tonio and Kathy slept through all the commotion. They were tired from the long ride from the army base. I really wanted to ask Kathy more questions about her past, but, since Tonio seemed so happy, I thought I'd let that go for now.

Chapter Thirty-Eight
Back in the Studio

I hadn't seen or heard from Amber in about three weeks. Meanwhile, back at the studio, I was trying to record some new tracks. The same night Amber stormed out of Mama's house, I had thought, if only she gave me some space, we would be okay. Maybe our relationship would be a lot better if we weren't under each other all the time. That same day at the studio, I made up a song called "Baby, Please Just Let Me Breathe."

Mikey and Tasty were bragging to me about how much fun they'd had in Vegas. The showgirls they described were better than the strippers in Atlanta. They said that they were puffing cigarettes with their pussies. I couldn't even imagine it. From the way they talked, I wished I could have seen it for myself. Tasty was just smiling at all the pictures they had taken with the showgirls. She said she wasn't ready to come back home. I think Mikey really did like Tasty, whose real name was LaTonya Mason.

No matter how late Mikey and I were in the studio, he'd have her sitting comfortably on the sofa in the room next to the studio. She was a singer who had gone platinum a few years ago. She was now focusing on other projects such as acting and producing. She also gave her opinions as to how my music sounded to her. We had known each other for four years now, and she

didn't bite her tongue. If a song was wack, she'd let me know before I recorded it. I admired her honesty because I wanted my music to sound good to the world.

One time, I had made a song called "Just Eat You Up." The words were too explicit. I had young fans and that song was just too much for their tender ears. I wanted to keep it though for a mix CD or something. Despite my lifestyle, I was still a role model for kids. My past with Daddy could have been a movie, and I'd probably win an Oscar, too. I wrote "Baby, Please Just Let Me Breath" for my next album.

Baby, Please Just Let Me Breathe

Chorus:
Baby, please just let me breathe
This is not how our life is supposed to be
Around each other 24/7
Out in the streets is where I'm driven
Baby, please just let me breathe

Verse 1:
You're always around me
I just can't focus and see
In your arms is where I wanna be
But your presence just keeps crowding me
Go to the mall or take a walk in the park
I think you need a breather, too
Yeah, that's a start
In the beginning, it was always fun
Now, I don't wanna come home
I just wanna run
Somewhere very, very far and away
But I have love for you, too
And my heart couldn't stay

Chorus:
Baby, please just let me breathe
This is not how our life is supposed to be
Around each other 24/7
Out in the streets is where I'm driven
Baby, please just let me breathe

Verse 2:
Being at home with you all the time
Is a draining experience and no peace of mind
Let's just take a chance and go our separate ways
Maybe not forever, just for a couple of days
Watch what I tell you and you will see
We don't have to be up under each other constantly
You have friends, and I have friends
Let's not let their friendships end

Chorus:
Baby, please just let me breathe
This is not how our life is supposed to be
Around each other 24/7
Out in the streets is where I'm driven

My album release party was pushed back for three weeks or so. I was just in the studio messing around to keep myself busy because Amber hadn't called me. I really wanted to call her.

She should have been cooled off by now. I had almost forgotten about the whole incident which really wasn't anything. I mean Tracy and I were only talking. I don't know what would have happened that night if Amber hadn't shown up. While I was listening to my own song called "Substitute," I decided to go to the local sex store. I went to buy me a toy because I didn't have Amber around anymore.

One day, I was at home, masturbating and thinking about Amber, Tracy, and Shelia. That was a hell of a combination. I almost blew that toy up. I busted all over that toy. Watching all those porn movies with Daddy had exposed me to some interesting characters, especially the women. Sometimes they'd just leave the man and go at it with each other. I wouldn't even watch the men. I would always focus my eyes on the women.

I still wore Amber's rainbow jewelry. I didn't want to take it off. I had it on all the time. I wanted to just pick up the phone and call her. I wondered if she had passed her finals. I wondered what she was doing at the very moment I was thinking about her.

Why hadn't she called me? I wanted to go by the school and check on her. I was beginning to really miss Amber and all the attention she had shown me. I wanted it now from anyone. It felt good to feel wanted. I mean, Daddy had made me feel wanted, but it was in the wrong way. He made me feel wanted sexually. While I was in a daze thinking about Amber, Tracy called. I let it go to voicemail.

When I left the studio and got home, I checked my messages. They were from Mama, Tonio, and Tracy. No sign of Amber. I knew Mama and Tonio didn't want anything because they were living up in Buckhead in that big house I had bought for Mama, but I was curious to know what Tracy wanted. I waited a day or two before calling her. We hadn't talked since that night when Amber was looking at us through the window. My album release party was coming up. I decided to call and invite her. *There I went making idiotic decisions again. Not knowing where Amber was, I called Tracy anyway.* The conversation went like this.

When she answered the phone, she said, "Well, Miss Tonae, how have you been? It's been a long time."

When she said my name, I started wondering what she was wearing. It was early. I wanted to see her in the nude. Damn all them pornos I had watched with Daddy. They had me tripping. I hoped that once Mama and I had gotten our professional counseling, the doctor could figure out a way for me to deal with all my daddy issues. Sometimes, while I was in the studio working on a song, in my head would pop women in maid's and nurse's outfits eating each other out like they were at an all you can eat buffet.

"I'm really sorry about the other night," I told Tracy. Listening to her voice, I don't even think she really thought too much about that night. She'd been with a woman for fifteen years. She was thirty-four. I was sure she had seen a lot while in her relationship.

"I just don't want any trouble," she said, "I didn't know you were seeing someone."

"I didn't get a chance to tell you because everything happened so fast. Well, her name is Amber. We've been together for four years. She was with me before the fame, but I think that it was something that I just jumped into."

I couldn't come right out and tell Tracy that I wanted to be with a woman because my daddy made me fuck him since I was 10.

"Amber is the reason I got discovered. She took me to this karaoke bar, and it just so happened my manager, Mikey, was there that night, so I kinda feel like I owe her. Does that make sense?"

Tracy really was a nice person. She looked at my and Amber's relationship from both sides and told me she didn't want to get involved until I worked things out with Amber. She even suggested that she talk to Amber for me. I told her that that wasn't a good idea. She told me that Amber had to trust me or there would be no

stable relationship. She told me that she trusted Catrice, who was her ex, with her friends. The problem was that Catrice eventually went back to men.

"You have to let Amber know that you want friends and that you want to see other people."

I told Tracy that I hadn't talked to Amber since that night. I didn't want to keep talking about Amber to Tracy, so I quickly changed the subject and invited her to my album release party. She told me that she could come because she was taking some time off from her law practice and her brother, Dave, was back at the furniture store.

I told her what time to come, and she told me that she looked forward to seeing me that night. I was ready to see her, too.

I went to Mama's house around lunchtime. When I got there, Mama was in the kitchen cooking, just like she did when I was a little girl. Tonio and Kathy were gone so this was my chance for Mama to give me the scoop on Kathy. She told me that they went out to look for a house. I had thought they wanted to live in the house I bought. I guess, since they were having a baby, they wanted their own place. Mama told me that Kathy had money from a settlement she was awarded from a company where she was sexually harassed by a co-worker. She was awarded $15 million. That's how she could afford that nice red Mercedes Benz. She was working at a company called Sentimax where they made toilet stools. I wished I could have won some money from Daddy for him sexually harassing me all those years. Anyway, Mama went on to say that they went to find a house in Gwinnett County. Mama told me that Kathy's stomach was getting bigger. She wouldn't know what she was having until next month when she went to have an ultrasound.

"Tonio really seems happy with her," Mama said.

But Mama seemed kinda negative. There were things about her that made me not like her, and I didn't even know Kathy. Tonio had told me that he was going to be a better dad than Daddy was. If it was a boy, he was going to make sure he played sports. He would be at all his games. If it was a girl, he'd be there for her, too . He'd be at all her dance recitals and cheerleading practices. Tears came to Mama's eyes. I don't know why she missed Daddy or cried at his funeral. He had fucked me more than her. I should have been the one crying. I would have loved to have been on the cheerleading squad. Instead, I had to be at home with Daddy playing house and shit. I was crying because she was crying. Then, I burst out laughing. She started laughing.

I said, "Why are you laughing?"

She said, "Because you're laughing. What's so funny?"

"I'm laughing at how fast Tracy ran to her car that night Amber came."

"Have you talked to Amber?"

"No, she hasn't called me, and I haven't called her. Maybe we are going to see who will call who first."

It was the night of my album release party. I didn't want Amber to spoil it for me. If I did call, she'd probably make me miss my own party. She had that effect on me sometimes. Like if I was getting ready to go out to the studio, she'd take off her clothes and invite me into her world, so I decided not to call. I kissed Mama good-bye and told her to ask Tonio to call me. I headed home to get ready for my party. I did have strong feelings for Amber; but, for some reason, I was beginning to feel that I wanted to see other women sexually.

Chapter Thirty-Nine
Album Release Party

When I got home, there were no lights blinking on my answering machine. What was Amber trying to prove? It had been two months. Neither one of us had picked up the phone to see if the other one was still alive. I sat down and thought about how she shook them dudes when we went to karaoke. She was so feisty. She was a woman of power who knew what she wanted. I didn't know if I should have paid attention to her actions that day because she did just make me her property from that day on. I was just taken by surprise when she said I was her girlfriend. That was a turn-on to me. Those guys had walked away with their faces cracked. That's what their asses deserved. Men always think women want them. Amber fooled the hell out of them.

It was about 5:30 PM. I wanted to masturbate and take a nap; but, if I did, I would miss my party because it had been a while since I'd given my kitty some attention. Instead, I decided to go ahead and get ready and get there early. I already had my clothes laid out. That was a pet peeve for me. I always got my clothes ready for the next day. I didn't like to rush or be rushed. Sounds strange, but that was just my thing.

I put on my red Versace dress with the black Versace shoes and purse to match. I looked like the star I was. I had to have on my Versace hater blockers. Not

only did they block Hotlanta sun, they blocked the mean mugs of people I didn't want all in my face. As I walked to my car, I felt like something was missing. I needed security. I felt like someone was watching me. I really didn't know my neighbors. There were only four of us on that floor due to construction. The development company wasn't done building, but I liked that loft so much that I had to buy it. I was going to ask Mikey about a bodyguard once I got to the club.

I was just doing too much by myself. I really didn't see the point of having bodyguards because I was a normal person. I just had a bigger bank account than most people. I was the same person. I still liked Wonder Woman. My favorite cereal was still Froot Loops.

My fame was beginning to make strange things happen. One time, while I was at Starbucks having a cup of coffee, I noticed a lady who kept staring at me. She was tall and pretty, but I didn't know if she was a crazed fan or what. I wanted to ask if she knew me. I knew she did because my videos were on just about every station. When I would look up at her and let her notice I saw her watching me, she'd act like she was reading a magazine. Atlanta was a big city where you could run into just about any celebrity, especially in Buckhead. Atlanta was the spot where it all went down. There was always something to do, always something to get into. Everyone did their own thing. I was just glad that God had given me strength and the gift of singing and writing. While I was sitting there, I got a real good look at her face. I had seen her eyes somewhere before. Could she have been one of Amber's friends stalking me? I had seen this mysterious woman in here many times before. When I was done with my coffee, the mysterious lady was gone.

When I got in my car, I let my sunroof back so I could enjoy Atlanta's beautiful weather. It was mid-

summer, so the weather was extremely nice. I arrived at my party. There were cars everywhere. The line was so long. Fans were lined up with posters of me. Some had on the rainbow. Some had rainbow dyed their hair, which I thought was cute. Everyone knew I was gay because of a radio interview I had done when my first single hit the airwaves. I wanted to be true to my fans from day one. Amber had told me to never be ashamed of my preference. At the time, she was right there with me, holding my hand through the entire interview. When I got out of my car, Mikey was at the door. He told me that a white lady was looking for me. He had told her to wait downstairs because he thought I was in some type of legal trouble. I told Mikey she was a friend. It was good to know that he had my back like that.

I went down to get Tracy. She sat there looking like she was going to a business meeting. I guess she just dressed like that all the time. I sat down on the stool next to her. She turned around, and her smile lit up the room.

"Well, hello, Miss Tonae."

Every time she said my name, it was music to my ears. I loved the way she said my name. She told me that a guy had told her to wait for me down here. I told her that guy was Mikey, my manager. As we got up to leave and go upstairs she said I looked like a million bucks. I said thanks and said that she did, too. We both smiled and proceeded upstairs.

Mikey and Tasty were popping bottles of champagne. I saw a big bottle of my daddy's favorite pop which had become my favorite pop, too. I introduced them to Tracy. Mikey stood up and said, "Let's have a toast to Miss Tonae and her successful career. I love you, and I hope we can have many more years together."

172

I said, "I love you, too, Mikey." I gulped down Jack. As we talked, I mentioned to Mikey my desire for full-time security. I didn't want to tell him that I had a stalker, but I realized that Mikey was ten steps ahead of me. It would all be in effect first thing in the morning. He told me I would have a driver also.

Tracy asked me to dance. I had a strange feeling. I felt like I was being watched, so I quickly eyed the crowd around me. No sign of Amber or the mysterious woman. We danced to my song, "Baby, Please Let Me Breathe." My body was there with Tracy, but my mind was thinking of Amber. I was thinking Amber was going to come and see me with Tracy for the second time and go bananas.

I had to give it to myself. As I listened to me sing, I sounded good, just like Patti Labelle.

I couldn't help but think about Amber and wonder where she was. I know she knew about the party. It had been advertised on just about every radio station. We sat back down and watched Mikey and Tasty dance to my other song called "Grow." It was a song meant for Daddy and anyone else who deprived a child of fun things like making mud pies, or playing hopscotch. It was also meant for a mother who had more than one child and used the oldest child as a babysitter while she went out or slept with different men. It was a song that everyone could relate to whether they were at fault or not. Because of how Daddy had done me, I didn't have a chance to grow.

GROW

Chorus:
Daddy, you should have let me grow
The love you gave me wasn't for show
I was too young to know but
I'm all grown and now I know, Daddy,
You should have just let me grow

Verse 1:
Growing up as a child was very wild
Being Daddy's favorite little girl
Would always ruin my world
So I continue to pray so my love for him would change
This heart filled with hate
Just won't go nowhere and escape
Daddy, who can I blame
This life I'm living is a crying shame

Chorus:
Daddy, you should have let me grow
The love you gave me wasn't for show
I was too young to know but
I'm all grown and I know, Daddy,
You should have just let me grow

Verse 2:
Mama, you had a part in this, too
Trying to be innocent wasn't the right thing to do
You knew Daddy was a monster in disguise
That's why I took care of you
Both to my surprise
All I ever wanted was to be a child
Mama, you could have helped my life be mild

174

Chorus:
Daddy, you should have let me grow
The love you gave me wasn't for show
I was too young to know but
I'm all grown and I know, Daddy,
You should have just let me grow

Verse 3:
Growing up as a child
I rarely had the chance to smile
Knowing my life was supposed to be different
I just knew love wasn't supposed to be like this
The love that I have in my heart
Is making my relationships have a crazy start
Being with people who I thought loved me so much
But it was just my body they were eager to touch
That's why deep down inside

Chorus:
Daddy, you should have let me grow
The love you gave me wasn't for show
I was too young to know
But I'm all grown now and, Daddy,
I wished you would have just let me grow

Tracy and I talked about what we had been up to. She asked me if Amber had called. Of course, I told her no. I told her I was going to call her after this party. For some reason, I felt Tracy really just wanted to be a friend. She really wanted Amber and me to work things out.

We got up to dance. As soon as we got to the dance floor, Amber came running toward Tracy with the biggest knife I had ever seen. It was too late. She stabbed Tracy in the heart as she turned around to see what was happening. Everything happened so quickly.

Tracy fell. Security rushed Amber. I was frozen.

I couldn't believe what I had just witnessed. If only I would have called Amber and checked on her. When it was all over, Amber left in handcuffs. She kept screaming, "Tonae, I love you. I did it for you."

Tracy was in a body bag. That was a day I would never forget. The day that was supposed to be a happy

day turned out to be one of the worst of my life. I cried on Tasty's shoulder, while Mikey talked to the police. She smelled so good. It also felt good being held by her. Mikey found out that Amber had a knife duct taped to the inside of her big purse. The security did check it, but it was well hidden. I slowly got myself together and went home.

When I was leaving, Amber's mom was at the door. She told me that she had tried to stop Amber. She even said she had gotten a ticket trying to catch her.

"Amber told me that she was very sorry and that she loved you. Please forgive her for her actions."

She told me that Amber had plotted this. I didn't know that Amber was capable of murder.

She went on to say, "Ever since her ex-girlfriend died in that car wreck, Amber hasn't been well. She has been taking prescription medication for anxiety and depression."

Amber's mom was so upset. I hugged her and told her that I had to get somewhere to think about what had just happened in the blink of an eye. She told me that Amber really loved me and couldn't stand the thought of me being with someone else. I knew Amber was a control freak, but it never crossed my mind that she could actually take another person's life. Mrs. Cooper hugged me and apologized again for what Amber had done.

Chapter Forty
Time Off

After the album release party, I told Mikey that I really needed some time off. He agreed with me and told me to take as much time as I needed. I cancelled all my upcoming events. I could definitely have used that professional counseling right about that time. All I could think about was Tracy's death, Amber's actions, and the look on Amber's mom's face the night it all happened. I had received numerous letters from Amber, but I wasn't ready to open them up yet. There was just no excuse for taking another human's life. Tracy was only a friend, someone who only wanted the best for me. She paid the price with her life all because Amber was so mentally screwed up. Tracy didn't even want to get involved with me until I resolved the matter with Amber. Tracy was a mature older lady who understood the mess I was in. I just wished I wouldn't have ever asked her to come to my party. I hadn't seen Mama and Tonio in a while. I decided to go over there. They had heard about what happened on the news. Mama had called but, I had turned all my phones off. I stopped at Starbucks on the way to Mama's house. When I got there, I sat at my same spot. I was about to order my usual when I saw that mysterious woman again. I began to think that maybe she was star-struck or something. I was fed up. I wanted to know what was with her. I went to the bathroom.

When I came out, the mysterious woman was gone again. I headed for Mama's house. When I got there, she told me that Tonio and Kathy had moved out because Kathy's house was finally completed.

I really wanted to go visit Amber in jail, but I was going to wait until I went to counseling. I made a song called "I Love Me Some She" because Amber had loved me so much.

I Love Me Some She

I love me some she
In her arms is where I love to be
Even at work or in my sleep
I love me some she
She's always around me
And sometimes it's disturbing to me
But the bottom line is I love me some she

Verse One:
Well, it all started out as a game
That she thought would be so lame
But little did she know
I wanted her from the get go

I love me some she
In her arms is where I love to be
Even at work or in my sleep
I love me some she
She's always around me
And sometimes it's disturbing to me
But the bottom line is I love me some she

Verse Two:
Waking up to her soft legs
And sleeping with her every night

Is a hell of a sight
I loved her so much and
The boys would say
Girls, y'all need a man and then we all can play
But no, no, no men are allowed when I'm with her
I feel like I'm on a cloud

I love me some she
In her arms is where I love to be
Even at work or in my sleep
I love me some she
She's always around me
And sometimes it's disturbing to me
But the bottom line is I love me some she

Verse Three:
She has a body and brains to match
The love I have inside for her is about to hatch
She loves me and I love her back
We're a good couple, the perfect match

I left Mama's house and went to grab a bite to eat. When I got to the restaurant, I heard a woman in the line talking on the phone saying she'd be home soon. The voice sounded familiar, but I couldn't see a face. When she sat down to eat, she had two kids with her. I finally got a look at her. It was Shelia, Shelia Jones from middle school, my singing competition rival, and the girl I'd had a crush on for all these years. I went over to speak and startled her because she didn't expect to see me. When she looked up at me from the table, she said, "Miss Tonae, how are you?"

I didn't expect to get such a generous hello. She still looked the same. She had two beautiful kids with her. She told me she was unhappily married to their

father. I had waited on this moment forever, but I couldn't come out and tell her that I had wanted her since junior high. We exchanged phone numbers. I wondered who she'd married and had kids with. I was so happy to see Shelia that I forgot all about my food.

Chapter Forty-One
Amber's Death

After I walked through the door, the first thing I did was check my answering machine. There were three messages: Mama, Tonio, and Amber's mom, who sounded terribly upset. I called Mrs. Cooper back first. I knew it couldn't be good. I couldn't even brace myself for what Amber's mom was about to tell me. She told me that Amber had killed herself. I dropped the phone. I immediately ran and got the shoebox under my bed that was filled with Amber's letters. The first stack read "I love you, Tonae" on each line. The next stack read "Please come and see me." The last stack read "I'm going to kill myself." I was overwhelmed. I left to go to Amber's mom's house. As pretty and smart as Amber was, she just didn't seem like the type who would take a life and then her own. When I got to Amber's mom's house, there were cars everywhere. Amber had a lot of friends and family that I knew nothing about. When I walked in, some people were crying, and some people were laughing at the fun times they'd had with Amber. Most of them were coupled up. I went to go find her mom because I didn't know any of them. I found Amber's mom in the kitchen with various photos of Amber at different ages. We talked for a minute. I was so glad that Amber's mom didn't fault me for all this.

We talked a good while. Then, I hugged and kissed her and told her that I would keep in touch.

When I got to my car, I noticed what appeared to be a business card in the window that read: Want Some Action. Travel available. Who could be thinking about any kind of action at a time like this? I don't remember seeing anyone in there that I knew. I had so much on my mind—Tracy, Amber, Shelia, and now this strange business card that just appeared out of nowhere. Amber had been on medication, and I had no idea. I wondered if any of this would have happened if I wouldn't have said anything to Amber on the first day of school. Could I have prevented all this from happening?

I went to Mama's house. Even though she hadn't been there for me in the past, it would have helped if Mama would have hugged me. I needed it. When I got there, Mama was in the kitchen cooking and writing in her notebook. I thought Mama was done keeping a journal. I knew, right then and there, we both needed to seek professional help. I thought I had read all I needed to know about Mama. I had to figure out how I was going to get that notebook. Mama asked if I was hungry. She was cooking lasagna. It smelled so good, but I didn't have an appetite. I told Mama what had happened. She hugged me, and I could have just went to sleep in Mama's arms. I couldn't remember the last time she hugged me.

Chapter Forty-Two
Counseling

I was sure that I wanted to go to counseling, but I wanted to go alone for the first time. I didn't want Mama to go with me the first session. I went online and found a therapist by the name of Dr. Theresa Watts. She was located north of Atlanta in Alpharetta. When I got there, the doctor and her staff didn't waste any time because they already knew about the slaying of Tracy at my party.

The receptionist immediately showed me to Dr. Watts' office. When I got in there, she had a big fish aquarium. It looked big enough to put a baby whale in. The fish in there swam so freely. It looked like their lives were better than mine.

I sat down on the comfortable black leather sofa. Dr. Watts told me I could lie down and prop my feet up. She was tall with a nice build. She looked like she was an ex-WNBA player. She also had a bright smile, possibly veneers. In her profession, she could afford them. I was paying her $250 a session. Dr. Watts handed me paperwork that explained doctor/patient confidentiality. She gave me a notepad and asked me to write down the most painful issues that I wanted to deal with first. All of this was painful. It all hurt. I didn't know when my heart would heal. No one issue was greater than the other. Daddy had fucked me since I was ten. I became a

singer. My girlfriend killed my friend and herself. End of story. Who could fix that? If Dr. Watts was willing to give it a try, then so was I. I think I needed three of her to get through this pain and agony. If I started singing spiritual songs, would it help? If I went back to church, would that help? I had only been to church for funerals— Daddy's and Amber's. I didn't make it to Tracy's because it took place in North Dakota. I wished I could have made it. Her brother Dave sent me an obituary. I did pray on a daily basis. I knew there was a God because of all the shit I had been through. I was still here. He loved me too because my dream to become a singer finally came true.

Anyway, the first and only thing I'd written about was Amber's suicide. That would be all I could handle for one day. I couldn't bring up all the drama with Daddy and Uncle Buck. In that length of time, I told her all about Amber and how she was possessive from day one. Dr. Watts had her notepad, too. As I spilled my heart out, she jotted things down. I knew she had probably already heard about what happened at my party, but I brought it up anyway. She asked me about my diet and sleeping habits. She knew I had been through a great deal of pain. She asked if I wanted some medication for anxiety. I told her no because I wanted to toughen it out. I mentioned to her how nice of a person Tracy was. Dr. Watts explained to me that they were gone, and she was focused on me. She deeply sympathized with me. She told me that some things that happened were beyond our control. Only God knew. I agreed because God was in charge of everything. Our first visit went well. I didn't want Mama to come just yet. I wanted to know what Mama was writing in her notebook. I wrote the doctor a check and made my next appointment for two months later.

Chapter Forty-Three
Tonio's and Kathy's New Edition

While I was asleep, I was awakened by my telephone ringing. It was Mama. She told me that Tonio and Kathy were on their way to the hospital to give birth to their baby girl. Mama wanted me to come and pick her up, so we could all be at the hospital together. We got there too late. Kathy had already given birth to a 9lb. 21 inch baby girl. Kathy was sleeping; Tonio was holding his precious bundle of joy. They named her Miranda Lashay Watson. She was very pretty with a full head of hair. Looking at Tonio holding her reminded me of how Daddy used to come straight home from work and hold me. I knew Tonio would never be like Daddy. I quickly removed that thought from my mind. In a million years, I knew he would never do to his sweet little Miranda what Daddy had done to me; for extra protection and since I was on somewhat of a vacation, I would try to keep her almost every weekend when possible.

Tonio worked all week. I'd get her on the weekends if it was okay with Kathy. I gave her a nickname. I called her Shay-Shay. Tonio didn't drink like Daddy. He only drank socially. I held my little, sweet, innocent niece. She looked at me with one eye open, cracking a smile at me that made me feel special, letting me know that I needed to protect her even if

Tonio wasn't like Daddy. Holding her made me think about my daddy's baby, the child I would have had if Mama hadn't taken me to the clinic for an abortion. The child that Mama thought was Bobby Knight's. She knew deep down that it was Daddy's. I started to cry. I went and laid Miranda in the crib and stepped out of the room to get myself together. I thought, *How could Daddy do something as horrible to any human being as what he did to me?* Daddy was dead and gone, and yet he still haunted me.

After I got my thoughts together, I decided to enjoy the life of my precious niece. I was not going to let Daddy's or Uncle Buck's memories spoil our moment. Miranda deserved to have all my focus on her. I walked back into the room. I saw Mama and Tonio kissing by the bathroom not far from where Kathy was sleeping. It wasn't an innocent kiss between a mother and a son. That kiss was a kiss like the ones Daddy and I used to share. Daddy used to put his cold tongue in my mouth. It tasted like death. I had a look of confusion on my face, but I played it off by telling Mama I had to go run some errands. I asked her if she was excited about her granddaughter. She said yes; but I knew, after seeing that kiss, that I had to get to Mama's house and get that notebook. I told them I would see them later. I left the hospital and went straight to Mama's because that kiss they shared wasn't normal. On the ride to Mama's house, I couldn't stop thinking about that kiss. How could she? If I killed Daddy, I could kill her. If her notebook had anything in it pertaining to them acting like Daddy and me, I was going to kill her worse than Daddy. When I arrived at her house, I looked hard for that damn notebook. My blood was boiling from the kiss and all the memories of Daddy and me. It wasn't as easy to find her notebook as it was back when I was a little girl. I looked

in the regular spots I had looked back then. I looked everywhere I could possibly think of. Right when I was about to give up, I went into Mama's bathroom and found it under her sink.

Mama's notebook read:

May 2000

> *I don't think I should go to counseling with Tonae. I don't even know how to act. I don't want to let a professional therapist know that my husband was my step-dad or that, as my husband, he was fucking my one and only baby girl. My husband was my mother's boyfriend. He did the same things to me as a child that he did to Tonae. When I was growing up, my mother didn't stop Tonio from fucking me. So how could I stop such a curse. Tonio was fucking everyone — me, Mama, and my baby girl, Tonae. How could I tell a professional therapist, someone I don't know, that I was fucking my son? We have some terrible family secrets. It all started when I was a child. I watched my mother do everything under the sun. I saw some things a child should not have seen, and I can't forget. Hell, I can't even forget as an adult. I did what I did with my only son because I knew that my husband was fucking my only daughter. All those nights they thought we went to bingo, we didn't. We went to a hotel on the Southside. How will Tonae react when she finds out that I've been sleeping with Tonio?*

That was it. I couldn't read anymore. I felt dizzy. I had to sit down. I was heated. I didn't know how I was going to kill Mama, but I knew I was going to do it. I couldn't believe what I was reading. Mama was fucking my brother. How could Mama! It was bad enough Daddy had fucked me. Now this? Her own son? I didn't

even think Dr. Watts could help me with this one. This was some sick, twisted shit. *Seek help, Mama. That's what you should have done when you were first with Daddy. Now, your ass gotta pay just like he did.* Damn, Mama was screwed up, too. She should be right next to Daddy, burning in hell. That explained why Tonio never really had a girlfriend when we were coming up. It was all coming back to me now. When Daddy would let me go to church with Mama she could have kept me the whole day. Instead, she brought me home so Daddy could have his way with me, and she could have her way with Tonio. That was why Tonio and Kathy moved out of the house. I had to kill Mama quick. Mama and Daddy were two sick individuals. That was why Tonio wanted to go to the army all of a sudden, even though he was good at basketball. He had even received a scholarship to go to one of Georgia's best colleges. Maybe he wanted to go to war and get killed in combat. Who knows? This whole family was just dysfunctional. I couldn't even deal with Daddy's issues, but I was on top in the end. I killed him for what he did to Mama, me, and my grandma, wherever she is. Poor Tonio. He was just as lost as I was. He went to the army to get away from Mama. Mama needed to die and go to hell. I was distraught. I didn't know what to do. I was going to kill her, but how? At least she had waited until Tonio was 14. Daddy had me when I was ten. The first piece of pussy Tonio had was Mama's. No wonder Tonio didn't have a girlfriend in high school. Mama was his fucking girlfriend. I was thinking about cooking her a meal and putting poison in it, but that would have been too obvious. Mama was the one who did all the cooking. Mama had to pay like Daddy did. I put the notebook back where I found it, left Mama's house, and went riding. I didn't even go back to get her from the hospital. I needed to get a drink. I

needed to get away. I needed someone to hold me. Anyone. I just needed to be held. I wanted to call Shelia Jones, but I was too upset. I just roamed the streets of downtown Atlanta.

Chapter Forty-Four
What Now?

I needed to get out, and that was what I did. I went to the strip club. When I got there, I went straight to VIP. It was not that crowded in there. I sat alone. A couple of girls came over to dance, but none caught my eye. I ordered a bottle of Daddy's favorite pop. I sat there for about an hour and listened to the music. I started to think about everything at once. Daddy, Mama, Amber, Tracy. I wanted to call Shelia Jones, but she did tell me that she was married. I was sippin' on my drink when, all of a sudden, that mysterious lady I had been seeing at Starbucks came and asked if I wanted a dance. She was the same girl I had seen the first night Amber brought me there. I remembered because she had won the amateur night contest with the pool ball. That was the same girl Amber turned away. She didn't want her to dance for me because she looked too good. She sat down beside me. I just looked into her eyes. She mesmerized me. I wanted to say, "Forget the dance. Let's go back to my place and fuck. We'll eat each other out because I'm a sexy ass woman who loves sexy ass women as fine as you."

We talked, and I asked her if she'd been following me. She told me no, but she had seen me in there with Amber. I knew I had seen her from somewhere before. She told me her name was Shauntae Green. Her stage

name was Spicy, but she preferred to be called Tae Tae. She was a stripper and had been doing it for five years now. She was twenty-seven years old. No kids and no boyfriend. She was in the lifestyle, too. We exchanged phone numbers. She kicked it with me in VIP half the night. I didn't want to go home alone. I wanted her to join me. We could have taken a hot bubble bath together. Then, we could have called it a night with both of us climaxing down each others' throats. I sat there for a few more hours sipping on my drink. I wanted to ask Tae Tae to come home with me. I knew she would have loved to because I was a singer who everybody wished they could be with. Shauntae looked like a porn star. She had on long eyelashes that made her look like she had slant Chinese eyes. She was light-skinned and thick like the stallion she was. I couldn't take much more of that scene. I wanted to make love to a woman's face. I didn't care who it was. I wanted to just bust a nut and forget all my problems. I told Shauntae I would call her first thing in the morning. She kissed me on the cheek as I left, and I gave her a nice sized tip.

Chapter Forty-Five
My Date with Shauntae Green

I called Shauntae before I even got up to brush my teeth. I just turned over in the bed and called her. I was wet from seeing her shake her ass all night. I wanted to spend the whole day with her. I didn't care if she was a crazed fan or not. What else could possibly go wrong with my life? I just wanted some love and affection. I had worn the batteries out in my favorite toy. I wanted to wake up next to soft legs like I used to do with Amber. I really missed Amber. I told Shauntae to come to my place so we could talk and get to know each other. I got up, took a shower, and ate a bowl of cereal. I couldn't talk to Mama or Tonio right then. I wanted to block them out, especially Mama. When Shauntae got there, she didn't look like a stripper at all. She had long jet black hair. She'd had on a blonde wig last night. She had looked like Lil' Kim last night. That was why I wanted her so bad. That day, she had on an outfit that looked like she attended a private school. She looked very professional. We sat on my sectional sofa and talked about her some more. I was sure she knew all about me and my demons. She told me that she had seen my car at Starbucks. Not too many people had my kind of car; plus, I had Miss Tonae on the front of my ride. She said she wanted to say something to me when she'd seen me but didn't know how. We decided to chill at the house

193

that day. We watched movies. She talked about her job as a stripper. She said she had started dancing to pay for college, but the money was coming so good that she quit school to become a full-time stripper. Didn't make much sense to me to drop out of school, but hell I did it, too. To each his own.

When it was time for us to go, we rode in her car. The stripping business was really good because she was pushing a Jaguar S type. We stopped by her place on the way. She lived in a nice gated community.

When we got in her apartment, she had Versace everything everywhere. Her whole house was decorated with Versace. She also had a pole in the middle of her bedroom. We stopped by for her to grab some extra cash. I was really impressed with her place.

While we were riding, Tae Tae asked if I wanted to go to Starbucks for our date. She was joking. She had a funny sense of humor. I liked that she kinda reminded me of Amber. We later arrived at this upscale swinger club in downtown Atlanta. When we got there, everyone had on masks. She grabbed my hand and led me straight to the patio. We sat at a table that was filled with a set of pink roses in a beautiful vase and a card with Starbucks in them. She laughed as I looked and read the card that said, *"Finally, I can have Miss Tonae all to myself."* She really had this night planned out. She had a bottle of champagne, but that wasn't my thing.   I wanted something harder, like a shot of jack. Everyone in there was naked and walking around like we were back in biblical times before Eve bit the apple of knowledge. I just sat there looking at and talking to Shauntae. I wanted something more to get me into the mood. I excused myself and went to call Big C, the neighborhood drug dealer. I knew he had something I could use to set the mood. Shauntae kept asking me about my family.

That just wasn't the time or place for that, so I had to call Big C.

I asked him to give me something that would make me feel good. Daddy's memories were starting to haunt me. I wasn't about to let Daddy fuck this up for me from the grave. When Big C got there, he gave me some powdered cocaine. I had seen people use it in the movies. Never did I think I would be doing it someday. He asked how much I wanted. I didn't know shit about it, so I asked, "What do you mean?"

He said, "How much do you wanna spend?"

"Three hundred."

"Damn, girl, you really trying to touch the sky."

"How do I do this cocaine?"

"Sniff it about every ten minutes or so. You might need to drink alcohol with it."

I had that part covered already. When he was leaving he told me that I might catch a drain, which meant the cocaine would come from my nose and to my throat. He said that was the best part of the high. I could tell he knew because his nose was running and his eyes were big. He kept looking around like someone was following him. I didn't know if I wanted to do it after looking at all his signs of drug use. I went to the bathroom and put my pinky nail in the baggie and sniffed away. It stung a little. Then, my nose went numb. I didn't know if I should call Big C or what. I realized that that was what happened when you used cocaine. When I got back to the table, Shauntae said she thought she would have to come and find me. I didn't realize that I had been gone for almost an hour. When I sat down, I turned the bottle of Jack up. I shocked my damn self. That cocaine had me doing shit I didn't usually do. I saw and heard everything at once. My mood started to change. I felt like I was ready to leave.

She sat there looking so hot and sexy to me. My pussy got wet looking at all them naked women walk by. We were the only ones who were fully clothed. I was having so many mixed feelings. One minute, I wanted to join the two Asian chicks in the corner. Then, I wanted to rip Shauntae's clothes off and put her on the table buck style and swallow all her juices, pussy hairs and all. Right when I did start to speak that drain that Big C had told me about came rushing down my throat. I didn't know whether to spit it out or swallow it. He was right, though. It was the best part of the high. I really wasn't feeling that swinging shit. I didn't know why she brought me to this club. We left and went to her place. When we got to her place, she just took her clothes off in front of me as an invite, but I couldn't move right when I wanted to. I kept draining. I was high as hell. She went to take a shower. I wanted to join her but couldn't. That cocaine shit had me straight tripping. While she was in the shower, I went out to call Big C. I asked him why I couldn't feel my face. He asked me how much cocaine I had done. I told him all of it. He said he was surprised I was still living. He told me to go drink some milk and smoke a cigarette. I had to settle for the milk because I wasn't a smoker. I checked her refrigerator and drunk almost a whole gallon of milk. When I went back into where Shauntae was, she was in the bed sound asleep. I was left sitting up in her bed, trying to make myself go to sleep.

Chapter Forty-Six
Shauntae's Company

I hadn't talked to Mama or Tonio for a while now. I'd been spending so much time with Shauntae. Even though she was a stripper, I was very interested in her. She had let me in on her little secrets. She told me that, in order to get the big bucks from all the other strippers, she learned how to make her pussy do little tricks. She did things like spread her pussy all the way open and make it beat like a heartbeat. When I first saw her do that, I was so amazed. All her customers liked when she did that. I especially liked it when she made her ass clap. I didn't care how loud the music was in the club, I was able to hear her ass clapping over it. Even though she was gay, she had a lot of straight customers. That was cool. If you were gay and you liked it, then do it. If you loved it, then be it. One thing I had learned was to never be ashamed of who you were and what you stood for. One day, while we were walking in the mall and holding hands, we got many weird stares. It really didn't make a difference to us. We had each other. That was all that mattered. We just kept holding hands. I had got very accustomed to the gay lifestyle, so it really didn't matter who looked at me funny. I was still thinking about Shelia at times when I was with Shauntae. I wondered what she'd been doing. She did say that she was unhappily married. It was kinda impossible for me to call Shelia

because Shauntae and I were always together. We weren't a couple. We were good friends who loved each other's company and had great sex together.

One night at her house, she put on some soft music and danced for me all night. She danced slow to every beat in every song. As she was winding her body, she made me want her even more. She was very sexy. She tasted just how she looked — good. When we were intimate, I never liked the strap on. She didn't either. That defeated the purpose of being with a sexy woman. We used to bump pussies most of the time. No need to get dicked down by a strap on. You might as well have been with a man. I didn't want a man. I'd been with Daddy all my life. There was no way another man was coming near me. When I would eat her out, she would lay in the bed with her legs wide open. Sometimes, she'd straddle her legs on my shoulders and enjoy me eating her. I acted like I sucking on a T-bone steak. I loved it when her legs shook, and her body trembled as I satisfied her. She tasted so good. Her pussy juice was just flawless. I loved it when she erupted in my mouth like a wild volcano. When it was her turn to serve me and make me feel good, she always took her time. She licked every part of my body from head to toe. I loved it when she sucked on my bottom lips and slipped her tongue in and out my mouth, Then, she'd lick from my neck down to my navel while sliding her fingers in and out of my pussy, putting them in her mouth and then in mine. That was not the first time I had tasted my own pussy. Shauntae's pussy tasted almost better than mine. She kissed my inner thigh, using her tongue as a tickler. It made me flow even more. By the time she got to the little man in the boat, I was ready to release and unwind. All that foreplay would get me to the peak of the mountain.

When I was getting ready to cum, she'd say, "Who's pussy is this?"

I would say, "Yours, baby. It's all yours."

It always sounded so familiar. Amber used to ask me the same shit.

Chapter Forty-Seven
All This Bad News...

I debated about calling Tonio or Mama. I couldn't believe their fucked-up secret. I really wanted to confront Mama and see what she would have to say for herself. How could Mama do to Tonio what Daddy had done to me? That was so unfair. If I killed once, I could kill again. Mama had to die. She didn't need to see another day on earth. It would be hard trying to kill her because she was not sick like Daddy was. She was healthy. Mama needed to join Daddy quick. I decided to go see Dr. Watts. I had missed my last appointment because I had been spending so much time with Shauntae. I had to admit that being with that girl had really taken my mind off a lot of shit, especially my dysfunctional ass family.

As I drove to Dr. Watts's office, I realized that I still didn't want to bring up Mama's and Tonio's drama. As a matter of fact, I didn't think I'd ever tell her. The damage had been done. I wanted to talk about Daddy. The receptionist told me to go on into Dr. Watts' office. I noticed something different when I walked in. It was her aquarium. She had only a few fish left. That was how my life was beginning to look. The people around me were dying, too. I sat down and told Dr. Watts that I didn't need a notepad I knew exactly what I wanted to talk about. I had already rehearsed what I was going to

say; but, just like the first session, when I tried to speak, I felt like I needed air and water. I felt like I was suffocating. I got a sip of water and began to tell her about a fucked-up grown-up game that I had remembered but never understood.

"I was about ten when Daddy said we was going to play a vegetable game. Daddy left the room and came back in with a brown basket filled with cucumbers, carrots, and celery. Daddy said, 'You are going to eat your vegetables one way or another.' I really didn't like Mama's vegetable soup. Anyway, Daddy told me that these vegetables would help me become strong. He said, 'We're going to get our nutrition together.' I didn't have a clue what was about to happen. Daddy had his favorite pop in his top left shirt pocket. Daddy said, 'This will be a fun game because we're going to eat our vegetables. Now, pull your pants down.' This was nothing new. The only thing that was new about this game were the vegetables. Daddy picked up the carrot first and said, "This will help you see better.' Then, he laid me on my back and slipped the carrot in my pussy. It didn't hurt too bad. Daddy's fingers used to hurt worse because he had really big hands. So after a minute or two went by, Daddy took the carrot out of me and bit it. Then, he told me to bite. I hesitated at first, but I participated because Daddy told me I was going to see the future. The next thing he did was grab a stalk of celery. He sipped on his Jack Daniels and ate the celery. Daddy liked celery. He didn't make me eat any of it. He ate it all. I was glad because that carrot was gross.

Daddy told me that, because the celery was partially green, I would be rich one day. Well, I am rich but not from Daddy sticking a celery in my ass. The last thing was that huge cucumber. Daddy said, 'This will get you ready for me.' That would happen two years

later because Daddy didn't have intercourse with me until I was twelve. He enjoyed me sucking his dick, jerking off on my favorite pajamas, and playing these fucked up twisted grown-up games. Daddy said, 'This cucumber is like a dildo.' The cucumber got soggy and crumbled up, so he said, 'I got this.' He turned up his favorite pop and began to eat my pussy. He ate all the seeds, the outside and the inside of the cucumber. Daddy ate it all. When Daddy was done, he got up. I looked at his face. He had seeds everywhere, and he said, 'Now I got all my nutrition for the day. Clean yourself up and go play before your mama gets here.'"

Tears were coming from my heart. I couldn't stop crying. Dr. Watts was crying too. She asked where Daddy was now. I told her he was dead. I left it like that. I wasn't about to tell her that I had killed him and that now I was planning to kill Mama, too. She wanted to prescribe me some medication for this unbearable pain.

"How could a father do that to his daughter?" Dr. Watts asked.

I told her that I was okay. I was just glad I had her to talk, too. When I told her Daddy was dead, relief showed on her face. If I had told her about Mama, Tonio, and Uncle Buck, she would have probably prescribed herself some medication. Dr. Watts ended our time early. I had fucked her up with that one. In her profession, I was sure she'd heard worse than that. I don't think I was the only girl in the world who had fucked her daddy. Dr. Watts told me that that session was on her and that she'd see me again next month. I didn't want her to feel sorry for me. It felt good just getting it all off my chest. I wiped my tears, got myself together, and headed home.

Chapter Forty-Eight
Strip Club Madness

When I woke up the next morning, I couldn't believe what I heard on the news.

Top Story: *Stripper Shot Dead*.

Shauntae had been killed at work the previous night. Apparently, there was a fight that eventually ended in gun fire. The confrontation was about a dance. One witness stated that one of the assailants wanted Shauntae to dance for him, but she was already dancing for someone in VIP. The two men then proceeded to argue. The one she didn't dance for left out the club, came back in, and shot up the VIP area.

"The police have no leads," said the reporter.

The victims didn't have a chance. Shauntae and her customer were each shot eleven times. My heart was completely shattered. I didn't know what to do. Everyone around me was dying just like Dr. Watts' fish. The bad thing about it was that the wrong people were dying. Mama should have been one of them people dying. Was I going to be the next person to die? I sat on my bed and cried like a baby who was teething. Shauntae was a sweet person. She didn't do anything to anyone. I had had so much fun with her.

I remembered one time, when we were at an upscale restaurant, she had the band play an instrumental version of "Let's stay Together" by Al

Green. I knew she wanted to be a couple, but I was happy with how we were. I was going to make our relationship official once I got myself together. Now, she was dead. I didn't know how much more of this I could take. I was a nervous wreck. I decided to call Dr. Watts and ask for some pills. I should have called Big C to get some more drugs. I couldn't grasp the phone to call either one. I just laid in the bed thinking about Amber, Tracy, and now Shauntae. I wanted to call Shelia Jones, instead I cried out a poem about killers.

KILLERS

Why and how do they get away
When one day they'll have judgment day?
You committed a crime and paid a fine,
But, if you ask me, you should have got some time
Doing shit that you know is wrong
When on that day, your mind should have been strong
It's over now and there's nothing we can do
But in my heart I'll never forgive you
Wrong is wrong and right is right
Whatever happened to regular old fist fights
You're supposed to be innocent until proven guilty
But if I find you you'll tell the judge please just kill me
My loved one didn't ask for this and that's fucked up
There was a special person in that life you took
She's no longer here with us on this earth
It was your mom that should have aborted you at birth

Chapter Forty-Nine
Tonio—Nothing Like Our Daddy

Even though I wanted Mama dead, I decided to call her anyway. After she answered the phone, she began telling me how big Miranda had grown. She said she was so proud of Tonio. She told me that Tonio had quit his job. Kathy had plenty of settlement money left, but she wanted to work. It had been almost a year since I'd seen either of them, so my niece Miranda was about to turn a year old. When I had found out about Mama and Tonio, I kept my distance. She called a few times, but I didn't return her calls. Tonio had called, too. He wondered when I would come to see Miranda. I didn't want to talk to him either. Why didn't he tell me what Mama had done to him? I should have asked myself why I didn't tell him what Daddy had done to me. Neither one of us could do shit about it. I bet those torn out pages in her journal were about him and her. Those pages I found under his bed weren't all of them. Well, it was too late now. I had found out. Mama should just kill herself so I wouldn't have to do it. How could she continue living knowing that what she had done was so bad? I told Mama I would call her later. I got off the phone and called Tonio. His words were kind of slurred, so I could tell that he'd been drinking. All I could do was think about Miranda. I immediately hung up the phone and went to his house. When I got there Miranda was

lying asleep on Tonio's chest. I knew Tonio wouldn't do the unthinkable to his daughter. There was a bottle of Daddy's favorite pop on the coffee table. It had become everyone's favorite drink.

He said, "Hey, sis, I'm just letting her feel my heartbeat, so she'll know I'm always here."

If she cried, he wanted to be there to hold her, to give her a bottle, or what ever she needed. Looking at him hold her reminded me of how Daddy used to hold me. I needed a drink. I knew Tonio wouldn't touch Miranda. Tonio said that he had lost his job because he was given a task and didn't finish it in a timely manner. Tonio was a foreman at General Motors just like Daddy. Then, Tonio started to cry, saying he had something to tell me. I already knew what he was about to tell me. I sat down on the sofa and prepared myself to listen to him. He asked me if I remembered all those times they were supposedly at bingo.

"Well, there was no bingo. Mama would go get a hotel room on the Southside. There was hardly no damn bingo. We went to church. We only went to bingo once or twice a month. Mama said she wanted to get away from Daddy and you.   It first started when I was fourteen. We would get a room, and Mama would turn on the nasty channel. She would say that we were going to play a grown-up game called 'Do as I See.' I didn't want to watch shit like that with Mama, but she enjoyed watching that shit on TV. Mama said that I was going to fuck someday anyway, so my first piece of pussy might as well be hers. While we were watchin' the girl on TV suck that man's dick, Mama pulled my pants down and started sucking my dick. She did everything that was happening on TV. She was sucking my dick and calling me daddy. She kept saying, 'Is this how you wanna feel, daddy? Does this make you feel good?' I didn't know

whether to stop her or to let her finish the job. It felt so good. I told Mama I had to pee. She said, 'Boy, no, you don't. You're about to cum. Just let it go. Fill my mouth up.' I skeeted all in Mama's mouth. She smiled and swallowed it all."

I looked at Tonio. He was looking just like Daddy. I was frozen. I couldn't register all that he had said, but I knew I had to kill Mama.

Tonio said, "Sis, I'll never hurt Miranda. This is my child. I'll always be there for her. I joined the army hoping to go to war and get killed so I wouldn't have to deal with Mama anymore. I realized when I met Kathy that I had something worth living for."

I kissed Tonio on the cheek. I felt his sincerity. I didn't think he'd do anything to harm her. I knew Tonio was mentally fucked up because I was, too. I knew right then, after Tonio poured his heart out to me, that I had to kill Mama.

Chapter Fifty
Mama's Gotta Die, Too

I plotted on how to kill Mama. She had to pay, but how? I wanted to see her suffer before she died. Then again, I just wanted to get a knife and stab her in the heart. As cold as her heart was, she probably wouldn't feel it. Anyway, I had to think of something. I called Big C and asked if he had a speedball. I knew that would probably kill Mama. I had seen it on a TV special about a man who had overdosed on one. He asked me how much I wanted and if I wanted some powder cocaine, too. I said yes because I wanted to be heavily drugged while doing what I was about to do to Mama. He asked how much I wanted. I told him three hundred dollars worth. He met me at the car wash. He came and sat in my car. He was carrying a gun and looking around like someone was after his ass. He asked how Mama was doing. I said fine. Then, he went on to say that, when I first went to college, Mama would come down the hill and ask for drugs. That I was a singer didn't matter to Big C. He didn't care. I guess, if you did drugs, you were nobody to him anyway. He said that, as fine as my mama was, she didn't have to pay for the drugs. All she had to do was suck his dick. He said Mama used to suck his dick like it was a crack pipe. I could tell Big C was high because his eyes were big and his nose was runny. I didn't even feed into all that shit he said about Mama

because I was going to get rid of her ass once and for all. He told me the speedball was darker than the powder. I opened up my little baggy and sniffed some of my cocaine five times into each nostril. I stopped by the liquor store to get the biggest bottle of Jack Daniels I could find.

When I got to Mama's house, she was in the kitchen cooking and listening to gospel music. Out of all the days, why did she have to be listening to gospel? It didn't matter. That gospel still wasn't gonna save her ass. I've heard that some people feel when they're about to die. Was that why was she listening to gospel all of a sudden? I bet she felt guilty about fucking Tonio all those damn years.

She had been writing in her notebook.

"Adding bills, Mama?" I asked sarcastically.

"No, Tonae, I'm writing a little bit of this and a little bit of that."

I wanted for her to break like Tonio did, but she didn't.

I said, "Mama, let's change the music for now."

I put on Betty Wright's "I'm Catching Hell."

I said, "Mama, let's have a toast. A toast to life."

Mama had no idea what was about to go down. When I changed the CD, I pulled the little baggies out. She wasn't shocked or anything. She even went in the kitchen to fix us some ice for Daddy's favorite pop. Mama didn't say anything. She just picked the baggy up off the table and hit it hard. And I do mean hard. I grabbed my sack and sniffed about eight times into each nostril. Then, I took three shots of Daddy's favorite pop. I guess Mama figured that, with all the shit I'd been through, I was bound to do drugs sooner or later. Mama was sitting there and singing along with the music. I was thinking, *Not yet, Mama, but real soon you'll be catching hell*

for real. Mama kept sniffing her speed saying, "This is some strong shit."

She hit it hard and it hit her too because she was high as hell. We kept drinking Daddy's favorite pop. I was like, *Damn. When is the speedball going to kill her ass?* My cocaine had a strange effect on me so I put mine down for a minute and took three more shots. Then, all of a sudden, Mama had sweat pouring down her face like a waterfall. At first, I was spooked. She tried to say something but I couldn't make out what she was saying. I really didn't care. As Mama was grabbing her chest, I thought, *If I call 911, they could probably revive her ass like they did Daddy.* Mama fell out of the chair. She jerked on the floor like a fish with no water. She finally stopped moving, and my work was done. Tonio or Kathy would find her in there dead. I cleaned up my mess, closed Mama's eyes, and went to the strip club.

Chapter Fifty-One
She's Gone Now...

When I got home from the strip club, my phone was ringing off the hook. It was Tonio telling me that Mama was dead. I wanted to ask him if it was what he wanted, but I couldn't let him know that I had anything to do with Mama's drug overdose, which I didn't. I just knew she'd probably die if she had a dose of mixed drugs. I started a fake cry and headed to Mama's house. I was still hung over from the night before. When I got there, detectives were everywhere. Mama was right where I had left her. She was on the kitchen floor in a fetal position. The house had a bad odor. It wasn't Mama's body decomposing. It was the fact that she had shit her pants when she was doing all that jerking and stuff. Tonio was crying and in disbelief when he found out. Tonio said he didn't know Mama was on drugs. I found that very hard to believe considering the fact they had been fucking just like Daddy and I. Kathy was crying, too. She had really liked Mama. I wondered if she would have liked her if she had known Mama was fucking her man. Miranda looked like a mixture of Tonio and Kathy. When we had Mama's funeral, it was sad, but I wasn't. She'd had it coming. Tonio and I were a sister and a brother who didn't ask for the cards we were dealt—a daddy fucking a daughter and a mother fucking a son. That was crazy. That was not how life was

supposed to be. I looked at Mama in the casket and wondered if her soul was burning yet. It didn't look like it. She looked like she was asleep. I thought to myself, *I did a good deed. Now, Tonio can live with his family and be happy.* How can I deal with all this that has happened to me? After Mama's funeral, I called Big C to get me some cocaine. That was what I used to keep my mind off of all the shit that was been going on. I needed to feel like I didn't have a care in the world. Mama was dead. She was not coming back. Those were the thoughts I had in my head until I met Big C at the car wash and got my drugs. When I got home, I called Dr. Watts. After about three rings, I hung up. I didn't want to leave a message. Instead, I called Shelia Jones.

Chapter Fifty-Two
The Girl of my Dreams

I called Shelia. She had no idea all the shit I had been through or all the shit I had done. I hadn't talked to Mikey. As far as I knew, he was still out of the country with Tasty. When I called Shelia, she was in court. She told me that she was a very busy lawyer, but she did arrange for us to meet and have lunch. I wanted to get me some drugs from Big C, but I needed to be sober when I was with Shelia, so I decided not to get the drugs. I got up and took a shower. I was thinking about all the shit I had been going through. Was Dr. Watts right? Did I need medication? I met Shelia at The Three Dollar Café in Lindbergh. She looked good as usual. We sat down, and we talked about her. I wasn't ready to talk about my fucked up life, so I let her tell me about herself. She told me that she was married to Bobby Knight and that she should have let me have him in junior high. She told me that Bobby had been selling drugs and getting in all sorts of trouble.

"Why don't you just leave him?" I asked.

She said, "I love him. Plus, I have two kids by him. Bobby, Jr. is six, and Barbara is five."

I never understood why a woman thought she had to put up with a man's bullshit just because they had kids together.

She said, "My mom went through a lot with me. I didn't have a daddy so I wanted to make sure my kids had a daddy."

I didn't see how he was a daddy if he was selling drugs and in trouble with the law. We hadn't been sitting down for five minutes before her cell phone started ringing. I assumed it was Bobby because she said she'd be home as soon as possible. She cut our lunch short and told me she'd call me later. I sat there and ordered my daddy's favorite pop to help me get through the day.

I was right. It had been Bobby calling. When she got home, he was waiting for her.

"Where the fuck you been?" Bobby yelled as Shelia walked into the house.

"I was having lunch with a friend."

"What friend? All your friends are my friends and all my friends are my friends."

"I was with Tonae."

"Tonae from junior high? What? Are you Miss Big Shot now because you're friends with a famous singer?"

"No, Bobby. It's not like that. I had seen her a while back. We just had lunch together."

"Well, you know that bitch is gay. If you fuck with her, that'll be the end of us."

"Bobby, you know I love you and only you. I could never do something like that. Bobby, she's only a friend. That's it."

"Well, all the dick I used to give that girl, how the hell did she turn out to be gay?"

Shelia later confessed that she had wanted to leave Bobby so many times. The first time was when she

found out that he was sleeping with this bitch in Englewood. It was their anniversary, and he did not come home. She went to Big C and asked if he'd seen Bobby. Big C and Bobby were the two main drug dealers in Englewood. As a matter of fact, they were rival drug dealers. Anyway, she rolled up in her white Bentley and parked in front of the trap house he was supposed to be at. She laid on her horn.

Some girl came out, screaming, "Stop blowing your damn horn before I come out and kick your ass!" She kept blowing the horn.

Finally, Bobby came out saying, "Honey, I'm on the way."

"What about our anniversary?" Shelia asked.

The girl in the window laughed, saying, "Anniversary? I got your man for y'all anniversary?"

He said, "Bitch, close the window and shut the fuck up."

When they got home, Bobby kept saying, "That girl ain't nobody. She's just a bitch whose house I work out of."

Shelia was one of the highest paid lawyers at her firm. There was no point to Bobby selling drugs. Her money was enough to take care of all of them, but he wanted to keep sleeping with this girl and that girl. Her kids were over at her mother's because that night was supposed to be special for them. She wished she wouldn't have ever told Bobby that her mom was a porn star.

After she had graduated from law school, she went home to see her mother. Her mother hadn't made it to her graduation. When Shelia got home, she went straight to her mother's room. Shelia caught her mother having a threesome. Her mother was getting fucked from the back by a big ass white man with a mask on,

and she was eating a woman's pussy. There was a camera crew and everything. They were recording that shit. Shelia had the diploma in one hand and a bottle of champagne in the other hand. Everyone in the room was surprised.

"Shelia, what are you doing here? Why didn't you call?" her mom asked.

"Never mind me. What the fuck is going on in here?"

When she entered the room, she dropped everything. The man kept fucking her mama, and the camera kept rolling.

"What are you doing, Mother? What is going on in here?"

"Who is this bitch?" The masked face man asked.

Her mama reached up, slapped him, and said, "That bitch is my daughter. Watch your mouth."

Her mother was a little lady, but she had a lot of heart. That man wanted to beat her ass, but he didn't. He apologized and left. The lady she was eating out was still lying in the bed. Her mama told them all to leave and that they'd finish tomorrow.

"Mother, you have a lot of explaining to do," Shelia said.

"I don't have to explain shit. How do you think your ass made it through law school? This is my job. I'm a porn star."

"Well do you like eating pussy and having sex without protection?"

"It's the nature of the business. Ever since your daddy left me for that no good bitch across town, I had to do what I had to do. When I got pregnant with you, he didn't want me to keep you, but I did anyway. I couldn't kill you. I couldn't abort you. Your daddy was one of the biggest drug dealers around, and I got used to all the

expensive shit I had. I wanted to keep it that way. I couldn't have you going to school with raggedy ass clothes on. I swore, when he left me, I'd never have you wearing hand-me-downs. I had to keep you in the best designer clothes and the best schools."

"Mama, I seen you eating that lady's pussy like it was an apple pie or something. Do you enjoy that?"

"Shelia, like I said. This is the nature of the business. That's what pays the bills. Oh, Shelia baby, come here. Give me a break. I did this for us."

"Was that big masked man just the nature of the business, too?

"Now, you wait a goddamn minute. That man is a good friend. He kept me out of a lot of shit. When I couldn't get a nine to five, after your daddy left, I went out to the streets and tried to prostitute. I solicited him. He was a cop, a cop who gave me a break. He said that I was too pretty to be out here turning tricks, so he turned me on to the porn industry. He could have arrested me; and, if that would have happened, you wouldn't have ever seen law school."

"So, what are you saying? I need to thank your masked fucker for my degree."

"No, that's not what I'm saying. All I'm saying is, since we've been doing this, I've made millions of dollars. He'll never fuck anyone without a condom except his wife."

"His wife!"

"Yes. She's about ten years older than him. He says the only reason he's with her is because she helped him become sheriff."

Shelia tried to understand her mama's point, but I didn't. They popped the bottle of champagne and drank the whole bottle. Since she had told Bobby about her

mom's profession, he'd say things like, "Don't let that dick-sucking breath woman kiss my kids."

Bobby left the house to go back to the projects to be with his trap bitch. When he left, she said one day he would get his. She wanted to call me. She didn't care that I was gay. She needed someone to talk to. She knew I was good people even though she took sorry ass Bobby from me in junior high. He was so fine and cute back then. When they first got married, he used to do stuff like run her a bubble bath and spend the evening drinking champagne. Now, they hardly made love. He couldn't get his dick hard because he had been fucking his ghetto bitch all night. One time, he even had her go to the store late at night to buy a Playboy magazine to try and get his dick hard. That didn't work. Now, they just didn't even try to do it anymore. She called me, and we arranged to have lunch. I was so glad to see her. She was still pretty. She had been pretty since school. She had lost a little weight since I had run into her last year, but she was still fly. I remembered when we used to compete in those school talent shows. We sat down, and we talked about the old times. I wasn't mad that she brought up the time when she ruined my dress for the talent show. That was because I had won.

"So, Miss Tonae, it's been a long time."

Yes, it has, I thought. I wanted to tell her that I had been crushing on her since the talent show. I figured since she knew my lifestyle, she'd give in. Plus Bobby wasn't shit. He couldn't even get a Wal-mart shopping card; but, let her tell it, he was her everything.

Shelia's phone rang. It was her mom telling her to come to her house quick. I followed her over there. When we got there, her mother was talking to a big police officer. Shelia's mom said that Officer Bell would explain everything. He told her that her white Bentley

had been impounded. He said that Bobby had jumped out at a routine road block and the canines sniffed drugs out in the car.

"I was in the area, and I called your mother. Your car is very noticeable. There are not too many people riding around in a white Bentley, so I called your mother and told her I had taken care of everything, including the drugs. I don't think you should be with that damn Bobby."

"With all due respect, thanks for doing this for me, but now is not a good time for me to be talking about my personal life."

"We don't want to see everything you worked so hard for to go down the drain over a petty drug dealer like Bobby."

I looked in Shelia's eyes and saw how much she was hurting. I wanted to grab her and hug her, but it was not the time nor the place. Shelia was a person who fought for the law. She didn't need to get mixed up in stuff that could ruin her reputation. We told her mom good-bye, and she thanked Officer Bell again. Shelia asked me to go with her to get her car out of impound. We got her car and went to her house.

Chapter Fifty-Three
No Good Ass Bobby

When we got to Shelia's house, Bobby was already there. When we walked in, he was standing behind the door saying, "Are there any cops out there?"

"No, there aren't any cops out there. Bobby, what's going on?"

"I don't know. I bet Big C put some drugs in my car. He thinks I'm fucking that ghetto bitch in the whorehouse."

"Well, are you?"

"Shelia, I don't got time for this shit. And why do you have this gay bitch with you?"

"Excuse me. I'm gay, but I'm not a bitch," I said.

Shelia asked me to leave and told me she would call me later. I had to think of a way to get rid of Bobby's ass for good, and I knew just how to do it.

"You need to let me use the other car so I can go straighten out Big C."

"Who is Big C, and why would he put drugs in your car?"

"Shelia, don't question me. Just let me go handle my business. You don't understand the dope game, so please don't ask."

When Bobby left, Shelia called me and asked if she could come to my house. She took Bobby Jr. and

221

Barbara to her mother's house. When she got to my place, she was really impressed. I don't see why. She knew I had money. But anyway, when she got to my place, I was happy to see her. She told me that she was thinking about leaving Bobby. Since she said she was going to leave Bobby, I already had a plan in motion for Big C to handle Bobby's ass for good.

I was sipping on some Jack Daniels. I asked Shelia if she wanted to sip.

She said, "Sure. Why not?"

I was a spider hoping she would fall into my web. Once Bobby was out of the picture, that wouldn't be a problem anymore. This was the girl of my dreams, and I wasn't going to let a punk like Bobby take her down with his life of crime. I wanted us to get intimate, so I asked if she wanted to watch a movie after she'd had about three drinks. She really was down for whatever. She said, "No, let's dance. Let's sing."

I said, "Cool."

I went in the bathroom to sniff some more cocaine. When I came back out, she was sipping and dancing to my song called "One More Dance."

One More Dance

One more dance is all I want
You're the girl of my dreams
I can't even front
Being with you has made me see
That you being in my life makes me happy

Verse one:
Most guys look at us like we've lost our minds
But you're the girl for me and plus you're so damn fine
We were meant for each other

And now you see
I help you out and you help me

One more dance is all I want
You're the girl of my dreams
I can't even front
Being with you has made me see
That you being in my life makes me happy

Verse two:
This dance will last all night
I'll dance to the beat and move just right
You love to dance and I do too

One more dance is all I want
You're the girl of my dreams
I can't even front
Being with you has made me see
That you being in my life makes me happy

Verse three:
Now is the time to tell you how much I love you
I love looking in your big brown eyes
And love your company
You got me mesmerized
I'm glad we met and so happy I'm with you
You're the girl of my dreams
It's like a dream come true

She was moving her hips. She didn't look like she'd given birth to two kids. She was still fine. I just watched her sing the lyrics to my song. I wanted to put her on my bed and go to work downtown. The way she was feeling she probably needed a good eating. I was just the person for the job. She landed on the sofa real hard. She was really drunk. I was more high than drunk.

This time, those drugs I had got from Big C were more potent.

I was feeling good, so I came out and said, "You know I've had this big crush on you since junior high."

She was smiling, saying, "Girl, stop playing. We was fucking the same boy. How could you have a crush on me?"

"I've been had this crush since that day you ruined my dress. It does sound crazy, but it's all true. I used to dream about you."

"You're serious, aren't you?"

"Yes, I am very serious, serious as my daddy's heart attack."

She told me that she was in love with Bobby, no good ass Bobby.

"He was playing both of us in school, so how can you say that?"

"What do you know about my life, huh, Miss Tonae? You're a rich bitch who has nothing to worry about."

I stopped her before she went any further. I said, "I've been to hell and back. I do have problems, too. I've had to handle my problems and deal with them."

She didn't know what I was talking about. And I had decided that I was never telling anyone else about my past. No one could do shit about it so I would let it stay where it was at—in the past. She teased me by gripping my nipple through my shirt. That sent a signal immediately to my clit. I was already horny from watching her dance. She was drunk, and I was ready to make her feel good. I asked her if she was ready for me. If she left Bobby, would she come be with me?

She said, "Yes, take me and make me feel good."

224

She was drunk. I knew the liquor was talking for her, but I didn't care. I just wanted to be with her. My dream was finally about to come true. We went into my room. She laid on the bed and said, "I don't know how to eat pussy."

I said, "Don't worry. You'll learn soon."

I didn't want her to do me anyway. I was just glad I finally had her in my presence. I went down and ate her like there was no tomorrow. She was moaning my name as I gave her my all. After she came in my mouth, she passed out and went to sleep. I wondered if she'd remember this shit tomorrow.

Chapter Fifty-Four
Shelia, What's the Rush?

"Why didn't you wake me up? What happened last night? I have a headache. Where are my kids? Oh, my God, Bobby is going to be so mad at me."

"Calm down, Shelia. Nothing happened that you didn't want to happen."

"What do you mean? Did you? Did I?"

"No. Take it easy. You were pretty drunk last night."

Her cell phone was ringing off the hook. When she finally answered the phone, it was a call from the hospital. Shelia's mom was sick. Shelia left and went to the hospital.

When Shelia arrived at the hospital, she was a nervous wreck. She didn't know what was going on. All she knew was her mom was there. She didn't know if she had been in a car wreck or what. When Shelia got upstairs where her mother was, the nurse asked her to put on a facemask before entering the room.

"Facemask? What's wrong with my mother that I need a facemask?"

"Ma'am, the doctor will be with you shortly."

When she walked into the room, her mother looked comatose. She was breathing with the help of a respirator.

"This is serious. She can't even breathe on her own," Shelia observed.

She couldn't believe it. Her strong mama was at the weakest point in her life.

The doctor walked in and asked, "Are you her next of kin?"

"Yes. This is my mother."

"Is there anyone I can call for you?"

"Doctor, please tell me what's going on with my mother."

"Your mother has pneumonia which is associated with AIDS."

"AIDS! My mama don't have no fuckin' AIDS! She's too old to have that shit! Take another goddamn test. Get another doctor in here!"

"I'm sorry, miss, but we have run several tests. She has AIDS, not HIV. She's at the stage where her body is too weak to fight off any infections."

"So, what are you saying, doc?"

"I'm saying that, in my 30 years of work, it's normal for you to feel this way. People are in denial at first. Then, the truth sinks in afterwards. It's okay to get a second or third opinion, but they're just going to tell you the same thing. This is tough to swallow. I understand your pain. You're extremely upset. Is there anyone I can call for you?"

She was wondering who she could call. Bobby was probably at his bitch's house, laid up.

"Yes. As a matter of fact, can you call this number for me?"

She gave him my number. All she could do was lay on her mama's stomach and cry like a baby. Thirty minutes later, I arrived at the hospital. I just hugged her.

"What's wrong? Why are you crying? What's going on? Are you okay?"

"Yes, I'm okay. My mother has AIDS."

"AIDS! But she's too old to have AIDS."

The doctor came back and politely asked me to leave because he had something important to tell Shelia. But Shelia said, "She's family. She can hear whatever you have to say."

"You need to start planning for memorial services because this stage of the disease is terminal. She's in her final stages. She has had this disease for some time now. I can keep her on the respirator, but it's not doing any good. Some people who have this have less than a 50 % chance of living. Some have to take a cocktail of pills per day just to get to the next day. Your mom has full blown AIDS, there is nothing more we can do. I'm deeply sorry."

Shelia and I just looked at her mama and continued to cry. The doctor didn't seem upset. In his profession, he'd probably seen that type of shit everyday.

I followed Shelia home. Once inside, we sat in the living room talking. Neither one of us said anything about the night before. Shelia only wanted to reminisce about her mama. Then, she broke down and cried.

"I understand my mama will die someday, but why does she have to die from AIDS? My mama, my own flesh and blood has AIDS."

We heard the door unlock. It was Bobby.

"Daddy! Daddy!" The kids ran to him saying, "Grandma is going to heaven."

"Shelia, what are they talking about?"

"Bobby, my mama has AIDS. The doctors can't help her. It's too late. If she would have found out sooner, then she'd probably have more time."

"AIDS. That's what she deserves. That fuckin' whore!"

"You're a cold son of a bitch!" I screamed.

"Bitch, I wasn't talking to you. I was talking to my wife."

As we began to get into a heated argument, the doorbell rung. It was Officer Bell. I left and told Shelia to call me if she needed anything. She told Officer Bell about her mother.

"I know, but I'm clean. I got checked already. Every time we made our movies, I had on a rubber."

Shelia didn't recall him with a rubber on that day she walked in on them in action. Her mother had even told her that they had unprotected sex. She was about to give the kids a bath. Officer Bell was there to see Bobby. He didn't care that her mama was dying. Shelia overheard him by the steps.

"Where is my money?" Officer Bell asked Bobby.

"I'm getting it. I need you to get me some more drugs out the evidence room like you been doing."

"You have already fucked up too much dope."

"I bet it was Big C who put the drugs in my car."

"Well, you need to get that bitch over there straight, too. She's fucking Big C, too. Hell, I've even fucked her. You can't be falling in love with a bitch like that. You're married."

"I'll take care of Big C. Don't you worry," Bobby said, "In the meanwhile, get me some more drugs. I
can move them at another spot on the Westside. I've been riding around all week looking for Big C. Don't worry, officer of the law, I'll find Big C and take care of him. Meet me at the First Inn on Cleveland Avenue."

"Bobby, don't fuck this up. Don't try to threaten me because I got shit on you, too. I have a gun."

"I got a gun? You think they stopped making guns when they made yours?"

Shelia couldn't believe her ears. That motherfucker had been giving Bobby drugs all the while. That was why he got her car so quick. She put the kids to sleep and followed Bobby to the hotel. When she got there, Bobby went inside. She looked through the window. They had drugs on the table. Several crack heads were in the room. They were in there testing the drugs. One of the crack heads even passed out. She didn't know if he died or what. Then, there was a lady who tried it. She smiled and nodded. That must have told them that it was good.

They gave her a package, and she left. The next thing she saw was very disturbing to watch. Officer Bell pulled his pants down. Then, Bobby went down on his knees and began sucking his dick.

Officer Bell said, "We been doing this for a long time now. When are you going to leave that wife of yours? I left mine. Now, it's time for you to leave yours."

Before they got on the bed, they both took a sniff of the drugs from the table. When they laid on the bed, they were in the sixty-nine position, sucking each others' dicks. Then, Bobby got up and bent over. Officer Bell fucked him in the ass. He was moaning like a bitch. When it was all over, Officer Bell filled Bobby's asshole up with killer cum.

Chapter Fifty-five
Is This the End?

Shelia could not believe what she had just seen. Was Bobby a victim just like her mama was? Did Officer Bell make him an offer he couldn't refuse? Did he catch Bobby selling drugs and proposition him the same way he did her mama? Either way, she witnessed Bobby getting fucked by a man, a man her mom had slept with who could have AIDS just like she had. She needed to get tested. If she had AIDS, she promised to kill herself.

"How long has he been fucking him? What if my kids have it, too? What will I do? I am going to get my kids and never go back home. Bobby is my world. All I am trying to do is keep a black family together. It seems like all these men are leaving their families, but I thought I was keeping my family together. I have enough money. I don't know why I have stayed with him so long. I love my husband, but I can't continue living a lie. Bobby doesn't love me. I knew he was sleeping with women, but men? That's a hard one to swallow. Bobby and I haven't made love in a while, but how long has this been going on with Officer Bell?"

She finally came to her senses and registered what was going on. She called me and told me that she had to talk. I asked her how she was holding up. There was a long pause on her side of the phone. She couldn't tell me what she had seen. She had to go get tested. If

she tested positive, she also wouldn't tell me. She only said that she had caught Bobby cheating.

"Well, isn't that enough for you to leave his ass? You're smart. You have money. You don't need him. You have a bright future ahead of you."

I had no idea that she was at risk of having AIDS or that I was, too.

The next morning, she went to the doctor to get tested. The nurse who drew her blood put on three pairs of gloves like she was infected already. She was nervous and shaking. *Why was this her job if she was going to be just as nervous as the patient was?* Shelia thought. She would get her results in one week. The doctor came in. He didn't beat around the bush. He told her that the statistics now for having HIV/AIDS was 1 out of 3. When she got home, I knew she wanted to tell me but couldn't.

I had the kids dressed up all nice. I had our whole day planned out. I prepared a candlelit dinner. I wanted to buy a gun and shoot Bobby in the head. How could he do this to her? How could he do this to their family?

When Shelia arrived at my house, I could tell she wasn't feeling good. She tried her best not to ruin the day that I had planned out for her and her kids. We ate the good meal. I had fixed shrimp scampi with mixed vegetables. Shelia and I drank red wine.

The next week came. It was time for her to go face the music. She didn't want to go, but she had to know. Her mama was in the hospital dying and Bobby and Officer Bell were somewhere skeeting down each other's throats. When she walked in, the doctor asked her to sit down. She knew from watching movies that when someone asked you to sit down the news couldn't be good. She sat down, rubbing her sweaty hands

together. He told her that on the last visit he had explained that one out of three were positive. She felt that she was the one out of three.

He said, "Shelia, you are HIV positive. I see that you're married. You need to let your husband know that you are HIV positive."

She didn't say anything to the doctor. She was just in a daze. She already knew what her plan was. She was going to kill herself and the kids.

She was going to go home, park the car in the garage, and leave it running with the door to the inside of the house opened so they could go to sleep and let the carbon monoxide take them to another world. She had been good to her kids and husband. Why did she have to play this hand of cards? This was a hand she had to play with no spade to save her life. She didn't have a deuce of diamond to cut the doctor's test results. She was simply set, set in the game of life. She came to get her kids from my house. We'd spent so much time together, but never I saw what was in her mind. Around me, she kept her composure. She only told me to come by her house that evening around 8PM.

I didn't know what was going on with Shelia. She seemed a bit upset. I was eager to get to her house to see what she had in store for me. When I got there, her garage was open and her car was running. I entered the house through the garage. Shelia and her kids were laid out on the living room floor. I immediately dialed 911. It took me back to when I had to dial 911 for Daddy. Not Shelia. Everyone I wanted to love me and I wanted to love kept dying.

I didn't know then why Shelia killed herself and the kids. When the police got there, they found a suicide note that read:

Bobby, you know I love you and always have loved you. Tonae, please see to it that my mama gets a good memorial service. I left you a check for $500,000. After you read this, I don't know what you might do. The reason for this suicide is because my husband Bobby Knight gave me HIV. The doctor explained that I could live a long time with HIV, but eventually I would be going to the hospital like my mama having a machine breathe for me. I'm sorry for taking the selfish way out. Please forgive me for this foolish act, but I could not see myself living with HIV that would eventually turn to AIDS.

Again I was thrown because the money didn't matter. It didn't matter that I finally found Shelia the girl of my dreams since junior high. All that mattered was I could have HIV. Before I left this world and joined Mama and Daddy in hell, Bobby Knight had to pay. My life was a living hell. I wasn't going to rest until I found Bobby and killed his ass. At first, I wanted to go get tested, but I didn't because I was intimate with Shelia. I had swallowed all of her natural juices like drinking freshly squeezed lemonade. My second thought was to go around like the devil and sleep with everyone. I could spread the disease, sort of like the devil in hell. When he got the key, he just went around the world destroying people, good and bad. In my thirty years of life on earth, I knew that death had no love for the good or the bad. I went to the projects to stake out the area where Big C and Bobby were trapping at. I wasn't sleeping. I was going to wait out there all night if I had to. I didn't know what I was going to do, but I knew his life was going to end that night. I was high on all the drugs I had been sniffing. I was wide awake. When Bobby came out the house, I followed him. I had my bright lights on. He didn't know I was behind him from the look of his walk. He looked

like he had had a few too many drinks. He couldn't see me. I rammed the back of his car. It went into the oncoming traffic. He had a head-on collision with a big rig. He died instantly. Now, I could die in peace.

Do you think a little girl like me will make it to heaven? I didn't go to the doctor. I took my own life. I couldn't live with AIDS. Everyone I knew and cared about had died.

The headlines read:

Famous Singer Takes Life at Age 30.

About The Author

Antoinette Tunique Smith was born in San Francisco, California and raised in the ATL, where she still resides. She is blessed with five beautiful children who are known as the five lights of her life: Pinky, Driah, Clyde, Chicken and Fat Boy.

She would like people to know that it doesn't matter where you come from you can be whatever you wanna be. Just believe in God. There is a God!

Thanks &
Much respect
Antoinette Smith